ORN AND THE REAL GIRL

Miranda Sapphire

Orn is a lonely orc without a clan, a tender heart who yearns for companionship but can't seem to find his place in the world. His only friends are his aerlanis, Gehyta, and the characters he writes and gives the life he so desperately wants.

Sara is a witch without her coven, desperate to find help in getting them back. The gods guide her to a remote cabin in the Kellaides mountains, where she finds a lone orc man full of surprises.

Their attraction is immediate, an all-consuming passion that won't be denied. But will the fire between them forge itself into a weapon against the evils of the world? Or will it burn them both to ash?

Orn and the Real Girl *is a sweet, fluffy, cozy ball of sex and nonsense for readers 18+. It is set in the same fantasy setting as several of my other works, but is a full standalone piece that doesn't require you to have read them. For those interested, there is a pronunciation guide and lore sheet located at the back of book.*

Tropes: Fated mates, she comes first (and often), he goes feral to protect her, he worships her, they rescue each other, found family, orc knotty times, orc/witch pairing, BIPOC rep, plus size rep, seriously gooey cinnamon roll MMC, sweet talk and banter as foreplay, cute animal companions, lots of fluids, a peen that just won't quit (multiple male orgasms), MF, HEA.

Triggers and Content Warnings: kidnapping (not shown), imprisonment of hostages (somewhat shown), blood, violence, mass murder (of the bad guys, not shown actively on page), threats of sexual violence (purely hypothetical, not shown at all), gore, animal cruelty (brief, only aftermath mentioned on page), snake pet/familiar, allusions to an evil eldritch-style entity, NSFW, fire which destroys a home (only aftermath shown), profanity, child neglect (in the past, and child is happy and healthy in the present), discussions of discrimination based on race (orcs) and vocation (witches).

Did I miss something? Shoot me an email (mirandasapphirewrites@gmail.com) and let me know!

For anyone who's ever been told they're too soft for this world. Your squish is your strength, not your weakness.

CHAPTER ONE

The Loneliest Boy

<u>ORN</u>

When I'd chosen this place as the location of my exile, I had made sure I was well away from any human settlements that might not take kindly to an orc settling so far away from the Fenns. There was nothing but scenic mountainside forest for leagues and leagues beyond the company I kept in my own home: my temperamental aerlanis—a long-necked wool-bearing farm animal—Gehyta.

Yet I always touched myself discreetly, fervently, as if at any moment someone might barge in and see me splayed out on my bed, cock in hand and body coated in sweat. It was the sole reason I'd bothered hanging a curtain to hide my bed behind.

Everything in me ached and pleaded for release, for me to wrap my hand around the swollen knot at the base of my cock and squeeze it as hard as I could, finally allowing tension to flare into pleasure. But I didn't want it over. Not yet.

I was just getting to the good part.

My free hand held a sheet of parchment filled with my own cramped, spiky scrawl, the well-worn page trembling with all of the tension I'd built in my body. I had many romantic stories

1

that I'd written in my years of loneliness. Even before I'd fled my clan, I'd been dogged by a feeling of not fitting in, of needing to keep myself separate from everyone else in order to keep safe. From a young age, I'd dreamed of love and belonging and peace, and as I'd gotten older and made my way into adolescence, then adulthood, my dreams had gotten more specific, more romantic, and eventually, they'd become…this.

I stroked my thick cock slowly, squeezing the swollen bulbous tip, flushed an alarmingly deep shade of emerald, stark against the more middling olive green hue of the rest of my skin. Fat beads of precum wept copiously from the slit at the top, easing my strokes and allowing my rough palms to glide over my feverish skin. I was having trouble focusing on the page, on keeping my eyes open and focused.

I let the page fall from my fingers, using my newly freed hand to cup and tug on my sac, trying to calm the overwhelming sensation of need. Even if I hadn't been the one to write the story in the first place, I'd read this one—read this exact scene—so many times I had it all but memorized, anyway.

The brutal Jeargan orc pirate captain Garesh had finally had enough of Corella Harrington—Duke Harrington's only daughter and a valuable bargaining chip in gaining legal immunity for him and his crew—and her ceaseless bratty complaining. She'd just shamed him in front of his entire crew, saying he was too cowardly to give in to her advances, into her pleas for pleasure to go with the adventure of being rescued— and then captured—by orc pirates. He had no choice but to teach her a lesson about running her pretty mouth like that. He had a reputation to protect, a crew to keep in line.

He'd sent her to the brig, had her wrists manacled and hung by their connecting chain from the hooks installed into the cell's ceiling, forcing her to stand for the long hour he'd spent deciding what to do to punish her. And as much as he'd tried to find something else, to avoid giving her what she wanted, he'd come back to it again and again, the thought haunting him so thoroughly that he could wait no longer.

Next, Garesh would enter her cell, broad scarred chest bared, his tight breeches doing next to nothing to hide his arousal. He'd been able to hear Corella's whining from the deck above, the grating tone of her high human voice causing pressure to build in his head like a thundercloud. When he unlocked her cell and stepped inside, tightly shutting the door and re-locking it behind him, he'd say nothing, letting Corella yip and complain at him with all the haughtiness she could muster—as if she wasn't bound and at the mercy of the Redding Sea's most notorious pirate.

Eventually, she'd realize that he was quiet and she was not, demanding to know what he wanted and what he meant to do with her.

Exactly what you wanted, he'd tell her, grabbing another set of manacles from the rack beyond the cell's bars. He'd bend to snap them around her ankles, over the surprisingly practical knee-high boots she wore beneath her expensive and impractical silk dresses. Once he was done he'd stand, towering over her. Her pale throat would have to bend far back to maintain eye contact, he'd be so close.

He'd see color creep up that delicate throat, see her pulse begin to throb faster. Challenge would light her dark eyes even as she tried to lean closer to him. He'd grab her chin roughly, squeezing her soft skin until it was dented so deeply it flashed white. *You're going to regret all your lip,* he'd tell her, and between one breath and the next he'd grab a fistful of her silk dress and rip it from her body.

She'd gasp, squawking in false outrage, chest heaving against her tightly-laced corset. *How dare you!* she'd cry, even as she licked her lips and pressed her face into his grip, fighting to keep back the smile he'd notice twitching at the corner of her rose petal mouth. *That cost as much as you louts capture in a year—*

He'd make quick work of removing her underclothes, his crew hollering and crowing as more and more of her tender

3

flesh was exposed. Unlike Garesh, Corella had never seen an excess of sun, or hard labor, or battle, and every second of leisure was made plain on her small, delicate body. You had to look closely at her to see the fire and iron hiding behind all that fluff and nonsense. And Garesh had seen it. Had been floored by an answering hellfire in himself.

Now bare as well as chained up, Corella would fly into a ladylike rage, calling him every nasty name she could think of, her chin high and shoulders as far back as her bonds allowed. She'd make it clear she was not to be cowed, that she was no meek, blushing maiden, as was their game.

Garesh would growl, grabbing a fistful of her tawny curls. *You talk too much*, he'd tell her, his voice all quiet menace in counterpoint to her staccato stream of words.

He'd lift her high enough to slip her wrist manacle's chain from the ceiling hook, causing a line to form on her smooth brow in confusion. *What was he doing?* she'd wonder.

Without a word he'd flip her, hooking the chain connecting her ankle restraints instead, so that she hung upside down. His men would laugh, barking suggestions in Orcish for what he might do to her. But he'd ignore it all.

He'd rip a length of satin ribbon from Corella's destroyed finery and tie it around her mouth, gagging her. It may have stopped her from speaking, but it would do little to quiet the human woman—in fact, it may have made her *louder*. Garesh would chuckle, oddly endeared by her commitment to the facade. Her cunt, now displayed for he and all others to see, revealed the truth: she was utterly dripping for him.

Garesh would take his time with her, circling her slowly while he stroked and pinched her most tender parts. He'd find all of the places that made her gasp and tremble, the touches that made the swollen bud of her clit twitch and throb from between her parted lower lips. He'd tease her mercilessly, her complaints eventually tapering off into panting and whining.

Her need would be clear. But Garesh would have only just

begun.

He'd bend, grabbing the chain between her arms and hooking, that, too, to the ceiling. She'd look like a creature being readied for the spit, but no suckling pig had ever looked so eager for its fate.

He'd undo his weapons belt, handing the heavy thing through the bars to his first mate Hellor, then stalk back to his captive, unlacing his breeches as he went. By the time he made it back to her his steel-hard cock would be free, flushed and dripping and more than ready for her punishment—and *his* reward.

He'd remove her gag, tossing the damp fabric aside, and cradle her head in one huge hand. *You'll take me now, lass,* he'd say to her, guiding his leaking tip to her parted lips. *And you'll take me 'til I'm done with you.*

She'd nod, her face red and her eyes dazed with lust. Her pink lips would part eagerly, but Garesh would have one more thing he'd need to tell her. *And if you need me to stop, to let you get some air, you clap your hands. Can you do that, lass?* he'd murmur to her, the words quiet enough that his crew wouldn't hear over their own noise. He couldn't let them know he was soft on her, after all.

Two soft claps would sound by his ear, and he'd grin at her. *Good lass,* he'd purr, feeding himself into her mouth carefully. Her eyes would roll back in bliss, her small mouth stretching to its limit to be able to take him. But she'd do as she was told, the faint moans of pleasure escaping her as vibrations along his tunneling length rather than sound. He held her head steady in both hands, pressing deeper, deeper, until he felt himself hit the back of her throat. He'd consider leaving it at that, but he *did* have a show to put on. So he'd press deeper, her throat constricting around his shaft, her eyes watering and the heft of him stretching her throat from the inside. She'd take him to the knot, fighting her gag reflex and eyes streaming, but there'd be no clapping. He'd fuck her throat slowly, luxuriously, giving her just enough of a break to gulp air. Her pretty face would be deep red and covered in saliva, but her eyes would still be begging for more.

She'd wanted his knot for some time, now.

He'd slide his cock from the wet heat of her mouth suddenly, her chest heaving with her breaths, and then he'd walk around her, eyeing her critically. *You think it's fun to provoke me, eh, lass?* he'd murmur, pinching a nipple hard enough to make her squeak. *You think this is all some high-flying adventure, is that it?* He'd stop once he'd made it to her legs, her wetness glistening in the dim lighting, dribbling slowly down her crevice to drip onto the floor. *You'll learn, today. I'll be* sure *to teach you.* He'd slap her ass hard, sending her rocking violently from the force, his handprint a stark red on her pale skin. He'd grab her by the hips to still her, angling her cunt so all could see her need. *See how she aches for me, lads? he'd* crow, stroking himself even as his mouth watered at the sight of her, at the heady scent of her. *Such a little slut, this one.*

Finally, all of the slow, aching teasing done, he'd drive himself into her welcoming heat with a loud, wet sound. Corella would scream, her back arching and her hips canting up to meet his. He'd stuff her full of his thick orc cock, her folds stretched tight around his girth, but her greedy cunt would want more, throbbing and pulling him in still deeper, begging with her whole body for more.

He'd set a brutal pace, one hand on her hip and the other wrapped around a creamy thigh, his fingers digging in deep enough to bruise, his claws pricking her skin and drawing drops of blood, but not once did Corella clap for him to stop. She whined, she begged, she howled, but she only ever wanted more. He'd feel her cunt seize and throb around his tunneling length once, twice, sweat coating her body and her face dazed with pleasure.

Please, Garesh— she'd pant, *I want your knot. I need your knot.* But he'd give her anything but that.

You'll have to earn it if you want me to stuff this highborn cunt full of my seed, he'd growl, gently pinching her clit between the knuckles of two fingers, pushing her past the moments of being too sensitive into the height of yet another orgasm.

She'd whimper, her whole body red and gleaming and trembling, as he withdrew from her, coated in her slick from groin to just above his knees, and returned to the head of her. Then he'd take himself in hand and finally, at long last, he'd squeeze his knot tight and roar his release. He'd coat her face, her throat, her chest, her small heaving tits, with his seed, telling her all the while how he'd hoped she'd learned her lesson, that from here on out he'd show him the respect he was due as captain.

And just at the moment that Garesh found his release, I allowed my own. The force of my orgasm sent cum arcing through the air, muscles so taut I bowed up off my mattress. It felt like it went on for hours, my body draining and draining until finally, the tremors faded and I stopped erupting.

Usually, there was at least *some* afterglow, some few moments of satisfaction before things went sour, but this time I was still shuddering with aftershocks when the dark, hollow feeling came to carve out my chest. It had been a good distraction, getting lost in the fantasy, but now all I could think about was how Corella came to adore Garesh, how he doted on her and took care of her and how *complete* it made him feel. And I ached, and ached, and ached, because I had begun to realize that I would never have that. I was alone in this world, would always *be* alone, and would never know the loving touch of a partner.

The puddles of cum all over my body were still warm when the heat behind my eyes spilled over, marking me as pathetic *and* weak. I laughed wryly. *At least I'm all alone, no one around to witness my shame.*

It had been many years since I'd been banished from my family clan—well, since I'd banished *myself*—and a lot of the time I was too busy to notice the old wound twinging. I had a never-ending litany of tasks that consumed most of my time and energy because being remote and alone meant all the chores were mine and mine alone. But there were days where I couldn't find enough to keep myself occupied, to fill my time from when I woke to when I fell into my restless sleep, and most of those days were in the winter. Up in the Kelladies Mountains, where I'd made my home, the winter stretched long, biting hard and testing my sanity as much as my strength.

Today had been one of those days. A blizzard had barreled in this morning, and now it howled and hammered at my modest cabin, making the rough-hewn timbers shiver and shudder like they, too, felt the deep cold. I slipped another sweater onto my body, doing my best to banish the chill from my bones without throwing another precious log into the fire; only the gods knew how long my modest supply would need to last. Vitrin, the winter god, was miserly with his mercy, and in many ways I was suspiciously lucky to have survived so long on my own, away from the care of my clan and the warm embrace of the Fenns. I snuggled deeper into my cozy layers of clumsily handmade clothing, saying a silent prayer to all the gods asking that my good fortune wouldn't run out any time soon.

Across the room, Geyhta bleated and shuffled closer to the hearth, irritated at the close quarters of my cabin and the meager heat of the low-burning fire. I gave her a wry smile, my lips stretching over my tusks. I strode over to her and crouched, stroking her warm, silky wool pelt and using my claws to scratch at her long neck like I knew she liked. She quieted, but I didn't miss the irritated glare she threw my way, wet brown eyes uncannily aware beneath the thick blond fringe that flopped forward no matter how I groomed her.

"I know, you're still mad that I ignored you earlier," I murmured, continuing to pet her to soothe myself as much as her. The wind howled and groaned through the cracks in my home, making us both shiver. "And this storm is no fun, either. But unless you've been holding out on me, there's no way to control the weather, aye?"

Gehyta blinked, her eyes studying my face, and tried to catch my sleeve with her blunt yellow teeth.

I laughed, yanking my arm away before she could damage the wool fabric—*her* wool, naturally, from her very first shear as a yearling. "Knock it off, naughty thing," I chided, smiling even as I gently swatted her neck. "Not everything is food for you."

She snorted, giving one more halfhearted attempt at nibbling my sleeve, then settled with a sigh back into her bedding. Gehyta was all the company I'd had since my banishment. I had tried mixing in with the human settlement in the valley, Thrul'hein, when I had first arrived, but my people were still thought of as mindless brutes by most humans. Naturally, it hadn't mattered how "well" I presented myself, how firmly I wore a mask of human pleasantries. My presence made them wary and hostile, so for my own safety I'd moved on quickly and only returned to Thrul'hein to pick up what supplies I hadn't figured out how to gather or make on my own. So long as I was quick and quiet, they tolerated my presence well enough to trade peacefully.

I swatted at the air like I could chase away such thoughts with just a gesture, then checked Gehyta's feed and that her water was still clean. I combed through her long silky wool locks, gently working out any tangles I found. I took as much time as I could tending to her, but all too soon she was clean and settled down for a nap on a bed of fresh hay, a thick blanket draped over her. I was alone with my thoughts yet again.

The longer I sat there, the more the aching loneliness from before pressed in hard and thick, choking me like a sickness. My chest grew tight and heavy, something darker than just loneliness slithering in, and I surged to my feet in a rush, knowing I had mere moments to cut this off at the pass or succumb for long days.

This was not the first time this had happened.

I darted to my desk, covered in sheets of parchment and used quills. The dozen cubbies set into the wall above my desk were stuffed with still more parchment, these rolled up into neat bundles.

My stories. It had started off as something desperate, one last thing I could try to avoid losing myself completely to my own despair, and I found myself returning to them again and again, hungry beyond measure for the comfort and distraction they afforded me.

It wasn't *all* wank material.

I snagged one of my sweeter stories from its alcove and unrolled the sheaf of parchment with fingers that trembled from something deeper than cold. Despair crouched just out of sight, a great dark beast licking its chops in anticipation.

I all but dove into my bed and began to read, my eyes greedy and desperate on my own graceless scrawl, awakening the fantasy I'd meticulously carved into the pages.

Maara was frightened and alone, I read, though she kept her lips clamped shut and her back straight, unwilling to show it. Her mother had gone to great lengths to make this royal match for her, and she refused to shame her memory by acting like anything less than a lady. It was not her mother's fault that the prince was so cruel. Her eyes met the deep-set ones of Sha'kith, the latest "present" from her fiancé, and she had to work hard to suppress a shiver. It was cruel, to make her use a servant so...unconventional, so inappropriate for a woman of her station. As if sensing her thoughts, Sha'kith's frown deepened, pulling his thin lips tight enough against his huge tusks to blanch. Maara swallowed, mouth dry, and went back to attempting to wrangle her russet curls into a passable style, rather than let Sha'kith do it, as was his duty...

I curled up tighter in my bed, piling my blankets around me and diving into a story I'd told myself countless times: a romance where a beautiful, smart, but overly critical highborn woman has her assumptions about her Orcish manservant ripped away, falling hopelessly in love with the caring person beneath those prejudices. I sighed and swooned at all the beats I'd crafted myself, delighting in their blooming love and their soul-quenching companionship.

If any other soul were to happen to see any of my stories I'd have no choice but to commit myself to death. Assuming I managed to survive the shame and embarrassment instead of perishing outright.

When I finished my story the night was fully settled in, the storm still raging outside as if it waited for me, a predator who had scented its prey and refused to give it up when it was so close. I peeled myself out of my nest of blankets to check on Gehyta again, smiling at her slack-jawed sleeping face and gentle snoring. Then I banked the fire and snuffed out the lantern near my bed. I checked all the locks and the latches on the shutters and my singular door, ensuring my home was secure against dangers in the night.

When I was done I stood in the middle of my cabin's lone room, licking my lips as I considered what to do next. It was late, and I *was* tired, but I knew from the jittery slant of my thoughts that sleep was still far off. So I sighed and returned Maara's story to its cubby, then considered which one I would dive into next.

I dove into my blankets, squirming and wriggling until the softness was piled around me *just* right, then unrolled the sheaf of parchment and lost myself in the story.

Everything was peaceful and cozy for long minutes, perhaps hours, until it was shattered by a frantic pounding at my door.

CHAPTER TWO
Witch Hunt

<u>SARA</u>

I was numb and exhausted like never before, pain trading places at intervals with a thick nothing that scared me. I was no longer sure that I was still alive, my spirit trapped in this hellish snow-choked forest, eternally searching. Searching for help, for something that I couldn't even name but that felt so *close*.

I checked the strange compass sitting in the palm of my hand, sending a precious spark of warmth into the shallow dish to keep the bloody liquid pooled in the center from freezing. The thin bone needle still pointed ahead of me, the sharp tip certain that ahead was the way to help and safety. It was a spell all the witchlings in my coven learned early, just in case. My whole body hurt at the thought of my missing mothers and sisters.

I didn't know what I'd find when I reached where the compass spell was taking me, but I prayed to the gods that I found it soon. I felt like I'd been slogging through this storm for ages; I had to be getting close, now. The stretch of the Kellaides mountain range my coven lived in was sparsely inhabited, but it wasn't *un*inhabited.

I had one hand holding my compass, and the other was

shoved into my layers of clothes to stroke the smooth, scaled spine of Lena, my sweet hognose snake familiar. Her body was far colder than I liked, but she shifted and breathed gently under my palm, her snaky thoughts twining through mine with little reassurances: *fine, am okay, cold but safe, love you much.*

I was trying to get us to safety, to find help somewhere on these godsforsaken mountains, but my coven's choice to settle someplace remote and uninhabited to avoid the wrath of small minds may have proven our doom instead of a smart way to avoid the persecution that hounded all witches.

Aggie. Mother Tonn. Brekka... My heart twisted painfully in my chest, the faces of my coven swimming in my mind's eye. I should have been with them, should have been there to add my strength to theirs to banish the evil that had found them and taken them. But it had been my turn to gather fat-of-the-moon, a rare mushroom that only showed itself in moonlight, and so I was gone when that evil found my sisters and mothers. I didn't know who *could* have taken an entire coven of witches. But for there to be no bodies and our entire hamlet burned to the ground they would have had to have been either very powerful or very smart. The gods knew that there were plenty of people in the small village in the valley below, Thrul'hein, who wanted us gone. But could any of them—even *all* of them—have done such a thing?

I felt so small, just one witch wandering the mountains in the hope that I could find something that would help. Since the bastards who'd abducted my coven had also torched and torn down our home I hadn't been able to stay there, even if I'd wanted to, to try and find them all on my own. I'd come to think though, over the long hours of my searching, that I should have stayed put anyway, that I'd made a huge mistake by setting out like this. But when I'd sought out the wisdom of the aether it had shown me the necessity of a journey, had shown me a roaring hearth and a feeling of warmth, of belonging—of *home*. Lena's little tongue flicked at my fingertips, a wave of support and love coming through our bond as she sensed the turn of my thoughts. *Good Sara,* she thought at me, *we safe soon.*

"How do you know?" I asked aloud, my lips so chapped I could feel them crack and bleed.

I know, was all she said, so I tamped down my irritation and impatience at her vagueness. She was a wonderful familiar, but she *was* still just a snake, after all.

But as time went on my doubts only grew. If anyone else was living on this mountain close enough to help me, then surely I would have found them by now. And if there was no one here, no stranger whose kindness I could call upon for food and water and shelter from the storm, then neither me nor Lena was going to last much longer out here. But the gods would not have saved me from one calamity just to end me this way... would they?

Lena curled tighter into herself, pressing her long body more firmly against my belly, and my heart shattered knowing I was failing her, my sweet girl getting dangerously cold out here while I trudged on. I lifted my numb face to the stars, concealed by the clouds and the snow, wanting to scream my frustration to the heavens, but as I did I spotted something ahead through the trees.

I froze, using my compass-holding hand to shield my eyes better from the thick snow and wind. It was weak, barely a flicker in the oppressive darkness, but it—

It looked like a light.

My heart stuttered in my chest, then began to pound with hope and excitement, energy flowing into my stiff, numb limbs for the first time in hours. I hurried forward, slipping several times in my haste, almost falling on my face, and that got me to slow down; I didn't want to crush Lena in my carelessness.

Through the gloom, a structure melted into being, a small cottage made from rough-hewn timber and slathered in pitch. The light I'd glimpsed proved to be a lamp, left hanging by the door, caked in snow and ice despite the flame behind the glass.

Smoke curled from a lone chimney I could just barely spot crowning the sloped roof, the smoke a slightly darker shade of gray from the rest of the world. I began to shiver in relief and anticipation instead of just cold and exhaustion. I was risking a lot by turning to a stranger for aid, being a witch, but if this person lived so far apart from the rest of civilization, up in the mountains where witches were known to dwell, then surely they weren't so easily spooked as the denizens of Thrul'hein.

And of course, I could always lie. Most people didn't have the skills to sniff out a witch, so why invite trouble by announcing it? I didn't like the idea of lying to someone I was depending on for kindness and generosity, but if I was attacked, then my coven would truly be doomed. I took a deep breath, bracing myself, and shot a silent plea to the gods that I wasn't about to try and solicit help from a violent criminal.

I staggered up to the door, falling against it with a heavy thud, and once I'd made one noise it was like something unlocked inside me. I was pounding on the door, shouting with my hoarse, near-gone voice. I didn't even know if I was saying words, everything in me desperate beyond conscious thought. Lena caught my excitement, uncurling a little from her tight ball to wind around my wrist and between my fingers.

I was so focused on getting the door open that I failed to take in some of the details about the door itself. Like the fact that it was huge, the top edge looming over me by at least one head but closer to two. The breadth of the thing would easily let two of me through shoulder-to-shoulder. And it was a *heavy* door, solid in a way I didn't think I'd ever encountered before, barely shifting or rattling even with me putting everything I had into striking it.

So, because I didn't notice those things, I was shocked when the door finally opened and a massive Orcish man took the door's place, enormous battle axe clutched in one huge hand and dark eyes peering at me in the weak light.

"What do you want?" he growled, and though I knew fear

and dread were the correct response, all I could manage was exhausted defeat. But also...

There was something else, something warm and fluttery, that was almost as surprising as the appearance of the orc himself. *Yummy?* Lena thought at me, and I felt my numb face heat up. I ignored her, shoving that unexpected feeling to the back of my mind.

I did my best to pull my exhausted body up straight, to lift my chin and strengthen my voice. But in the end all I could manage were four words in a soft rasp: "Please. I need...help."

CHAPTER THREE

The Real Girl

ORN

The last thing I'd expected when I'd opened my door was a small human woman. She looked half-dead, bundled in layers of clothes and with a satchel slung across her chest. One hand clutched at my doorway, the other buried in her layers to clutch at her belly. *An injury?* I wondered with a sharp spike of panic. The gods knew I was no healer, and there was no one else for leagues; if it was up to me to keep this woman alive, then she might have been better off taking her chances with the wolves.

Another strong gust of bitter-cold wind blasted into us, and the woman staggered forward, sagging at the threshold, and I moved to catch her without thinking. My axe clattered to the ground, but I managed to keep the woman more or less upright.

"I..." she whispered, her large brown eyes dazed and heavily bruised with fatigue. "I need....help."

I swallowed hard, my mouth and throat dry enough to ache, then hauled her up and cradled her carefully in my arms, balancing her weight so that I could use an arm to shoulder the heavy ironwood door shut.

"Of course you do," I told her, shaking with nerves and something else I had no name for, something that made me feel flushed and cold at the same time. I did my best to ignore the feeling, striding across the room and kicking a stool closer to the fire. The noise startled Gehyta awake with a camelid bleat, her triangular ears flattening in concern. I set the woman gingerly onto the wooden stool. "I have no gift for healing," I warned her, taking my kettle and hanging it over the fire. I stoked the flames back to life, adding two precious logs to get it nice and hot. If I needed to chop more wood in a blizzard, then so be it; I wasn't going to let this stranger freeze to death."But you're welcome to my supplies. Anything you need."

A small part of me was horrified by my recklessness, letting a stranger into my home like this and giving her unfettered access to whatever she wanted. For all I knew, she could be here to kill me and rob me, her plea for help a ruse to get my guard down. My older siblings had always told me I trusted too easily, and this could very well be the time it cost me something I couldn't replace. But most of me was eager to give her whatever she needed, something about this haggard stranger making my blood sing, making me okay with the risk in trusting her.

The woman blinked up at me, her warm brown complexion wan and pale even with the golden cast of the fire liming her heart-shaped face. I realized with a lurch that she was quite beautiful, even looking halfway to the gods and nearly frozen. My face heated and I spun away from her, scurrying all over my little kitchen area to get her tea and something to eat. My reactions were scaring me, but the act of getting a guest settled and fed soothed away the worst of it.

My heart settled and my face felt less obviously flushed when I went to my wardrobe and pulled out sweaters and a pair of leggings, knowing my mystery guest needed to get out of her cold wet clothes if she was to have any chance of warming up. I returned to her side and held out my offering to her awkwardly. "None of this will fit you, but i-it's at least warm and dry.

So...have at it," I mumbled.

Her head cocked, her delicate brows furrowing. "I don't know if I can move," she said at last, swallowing hard, and I dove for my water jug to get her a drink. I felt like an idiot for not giving her water right away. She took a long drink, wincing a little but sighing with satisfaction when she was done. She handed the empty cup back to me and I had to squash an insane urge to lick the rim where she'd drunk from it. Suddenly, my mind was drifting to the carnal places it had been sunk in all night with my lewd stories, and to my horror my body was reacting. I worked so hard to stuff those thoughts to the back of my mind that I almost stumbled from the mental effort.

"Can I ask you to help me?" she ventured, her voice smoother and richer after her drink. Hearing her speak was like being wrapped up in smoke and honey, and I shivered with pleasure to hear it.

It took a moment for me to realize what she was asking for, and when the dots connected all my hard work gaining control of myself went to out the window. The idea of having my hands on her body made me weak in the knees, but she needed help, not some lonely star-struck orc drooling and ogling her when she was unwell and vulnerable. I was stronger than my base urges, and with a deep breath, I cleared my mind. I nodded, holding my hands out for her to take so I could help her back to her feet. She swayed and wobbled badly once she was up, but after a moment managed to get her feet under her and stand unassisted. But it was clear to me that I would be doing most of the work. That sobered me further, cooling the flames of my inexplicable ardor.

I swallowed, licking my lips, then reached out with badly trembling hands to help her undress. The first two layers were coats, both sodden, that I tossed onto my table to hang later. Then she had a thick sweater, and when I told her to lift her arms up so I could peel it off of her shivering body, something shifted and *moved* against her belly, and I felt faint for a moment. *Gods above and below, please let that not be her insides trying to be outsides,* I prayed, freezing with her damp sweater clutched in my hands as I watched the movement.

It took a moment, but eventually she noticed my stare and smiled weakly. "'S'all right," she said, lifting her tunic to reveal an expanse of soft, round brown stomach—and a snake, shimmering black in color and flicking its tongue at me curiously from where it was curled around the woman's torso like a living belt. I started, surprised by such a strange companion, but it was just a little hognose, harmless, so I threw her sweater aside as well and pressed on. I mused that having a snake for a pet in the cold of the mountains felt like a foolish choice, but then again, I'd been having complete one-sided conversations with Gehyta for years, so who was I to judge?

The woman coaxed the snake onto her arm, murmuring soft things to it and petting its little diamond-shaped head. She indicated I could proceed, and I carefully helped her out of her last layer of clothes, until she stood before me in just her smallclothes, miles of rich brown skin and delicious curves on display. *She's hurt and on death's door,* I chided myself, angry at my juvenile reactions to her beauty and her closeness. I ripped my gaze away from her tantalizing form and began helping her into the clothes I'd grabbed, starting with the leggings. She had to grip my shoulders to steady herself enough to step into them, and I couldn't quite control the hitch in my breath at the feel of her little hands on me. *You're too full of romantic nonsense, Orn. The chance she'd want you are slim,* I told myself, grabbing a spare tunic next. *She's human, and you're an orc. A* clanless *orc, even. Keep your head about you, man!*

I tried to keep my skin from touching hers as much as I could while I got her dressed, not wanting to overstep my bounds or rile myself up too much more. Her snake disappeared under her clothes to warm up once I was done. I was saved from having to figure out what to say by the kettle whistling, and I hurried to make her tea with more haste than was necessary. I considered re-heating my leftover stew from dinner to give to her, but I'd heard that humans didn't like Orcish spices, so I plated some bread and a little hard cheese for her instead.

Gehyta watched us from where she was lying on the floor, nonchalantly chewing at some of the hay I'd piled up for her bedding. She'd always been a bit skittish, even by aerlanis standards, but she was surprisingly calm in the face of an unknown person. Strange, that—and still more strange that she wasn't infected by my nerves.

When the tea was ready, I handed it to my guest, her small brown hands impossibly tiny against my earthenware mug, and she took a careful sip. She closed her eyes and moaned, shivering once, before her eyes peeled open and caught mine. "This is really good!" she said, some color back in her face already. "What's in this?"

I shrugged, settling into a crouch so I could cover my nerves by pretending to care for my sleeping aerlanis. I reached over and buried my fingers in Gehyta's silky pelt, earning me a bleary look of disdain before the aerlanis settled once more. "It's a blend from the Fenns," I told her slowly, my mind suddenly devoid of any singular thing that was in that tea. But it did odd things to my chest to see her enjoying something that I'd given her so much.

"It's lovely. So spicy!" She hummed in contentment, taking another sip. "It's warming me up like a good whiskey."

"I have some of that too, if you want."

She shook her head, something passing over her soft features that I couldn't quite read. "No, that's fine. You've already been so kind." She started, her eyes darting to my face and going wide. "Bloody gods, I never even introduced myself!" She held out one of her dainty hands and smiled at me. "My name is Sara. And my...my pet is called Lena."

I took her hand, careful of my grip, and my breath caught at the feel of her skin on mine, like a bolt of lightning fizzing up my spine. The fine hairs on my body stood on end, and I licked my lips, nervous and self-conscious despite Sara's friendliness. "I'm Orn—" I almost kept going, giving my clan name, despite not having had any claim to their kinship for several years now. "Just Orn" I finished lamely. I busied myself with standing and fetching my other stool. I should probably try to give Sara privacy and space now that she was settling in, but I was unable to tamp down the hope that she'd want to keep talking to me, to maybe even be something of a friend while she recuperated. "What, um...what brings you so far from civilization?" I asked.

She bit her lip, her gaze going flat and distant in a way that made me panic. "N-not that you have to tell me your business!" I added hurriedly, my face so hot I was certain my skin was a moment from melting clean off of my skull. "I was—um, that is, I was just curious. Trying to make conversation—" Gods, did that high-pitched giggle come from *me?* I was mere moments from throwing myself into a snow drift outside and letting Frichta guide my soul to the hereafter.

Sara managed a small smile, reaching out to grasp one of my flailing hands. "It's alright, Orn, I know you didn't mean anything by it. You're a very kind and considerate person." She sighed, releasing me, and her snake Lena poked her tiny head out of the collar of Sara's borrowed clothes, the rest of her following gradually to twine around Sara's head like a strange hat, tousling her long dark curls. "I'm just not...I-I can't talk about it, just yet. I swear to you though, I mean you no harm."

I nearly laughed at the last bit; since when did a lone human woman feel the need to reassure a fully-grown orc that she wasn't a threat? Her delicate limbs and soft human skin said that loud and clear. But from Sara's expression, she had clearly come from something bad, something that she was struggling to make sense of, so perhaps that was why she said such odd things. I was troubled by what could have befallen her, angry that someone so beautiful and sweet should suffer, but I was also perversely glad that whatever had happened had guided her to my cottage for help.

Suddenly, her mouth split in a jaw-cracking yawn, and I surged to my feet once more, my eyes darting over my small home in a panic. Vitrin's mercy, where would she *sleep*?

My gaze landed on my bed, and I decided in a flash that it was all hers. But it was too far from the fire—I tended to run hot in my sleep, so I kept it as far from the hearth as possible—so I hurried over to drag it closer. The feet squealed and scraped against my carefully laid plank floor, but the ironwood frame was too heavy for me to lift properly by myself. Sara watched me, bemused, Lena's little snub-nosed face turned to me and also watching. I finished dragging the bed over, leaving enough distance between it and the flames to avoid errant sparks and embers, then pointed at it.

"You'll sleep here," I told her, taking the largest blanket from the unkempt pile and spreading it on the floor over some of Gehyta's clean hay. "You should sleep now. Unless you need something else?"

Sara blinked, looking between me and the empty bed. "I can't take your bed," she protested, biting her lip again. "You've already done so much, Orn"

"Well, *I'm* not sleeping in it," I told her, internally wincing when I heard how sharp that sounded. "And Gehyta gets nervous around strangers, so it's best for me to sleep on the floor by her, anyway." I gestured at Gehyta, who had never looked so calm and placid before in her entire life, I was certain. I coughed. "So...so you might as well."

She hesitated for another few seconds, then sighed and rolled her eyes, smiling at me. "Fine, have it your way. I'm too tired to argue. But I don't believe you for a second," she winked, sinking into the mattress and rearranging the piles of blankets around her much smaller body.

I settled into my new bed, Gehyta uncurling a little to lay her head on my chest, making contented little snorts and huffs as I scratched behind her thick, triangular ears and down her soft muzzle.

Even though I should have been exhausted, my body was too tense and humming with nerves to settle into sleep. The whole evening felt surreal, like a fever dream, but even if my mind was struggling to accept the reality of Sara's arrival, my body was not. Every inch of me felt hot and oversensitive, my cock stuck half-hard no matter how much I tried to calm it down. Something teased at the back of my mind, a vague memory that felt relevant to this situation, but whenever I tried to focus on it, it darted away. I cursed silently, wishing I were still in the Fenns and could ask for guidance from my clan.

I may have been having trouble drifting off, but it wasn't long before I heard Sara's breathing slow and deepen into an even rhythm. And then, much to my surprise, she began to snore—*loudly*. The sound woke Gehyta from her own slumber with a disgruntled snort, but I only smiled, oddly charmed.

Eventually, sleep found me, though it was troubled by odd dreams that constantly shifted and changed. I didn't remember any of them when I woke with the dawn.

CHAPTER FOUR

Breakfast In Bed

<u>SARA</u>

My dreams were full of hopeless searching, but when I woke up I felt refreshed anyway. The smell of ham and eggs cooking filled the air, and my stomach gave a mighty heave and a roar, the bread and cheese from last night utterly spent. I was so focused on the delicious smells and the comfortable nest I found myself in that it took a moment for memory to trickle in and remind me where I was.

To remember Orn.

I was in an orc's cottage, imposing on his kindness and hospitality, because... Tears burned at the backs of my eyes, threatening to spill, so I stuffed those memories down to pick over later, because I didn't have time to break down. My coven needed me. I had to focus on getting back on my feet and figuring out my next steps, on finding them and rescuing them before it was too late. If it wasn't already—

No. No. Bad, Sara. Stay away from these sorts of thoughts.

I frowned and sat up, rubbing a heavy crust from my eyes and the side of my mouth—sweet Delenaa, had I been drooling in my sleep?—and smiled at the sight of Orn hunched over his breakfast at the nearby table. It wasn't much lighter inside his cabin now that it was daytime, but it was bright enough that I could see just how handsome my host was. The tusks had thrown me off at first, but the lips that surrounded them were well-formed and plush, and now that I'd been looking at him awhile, those tusks didn't stick out to me any more than anything else about him did. His features were so bold they verged on harsh, but they were balanced well, and the warmth in his dark eyes held me like a snare, tempting me to get closer, to sink into those eyes and let myself swim.

Oh fuck, I'm staring.

He swallowed heavily when he noticed me studying him and grinning like a lunatic, but then he smiled back, his deep green lips stretched thin over his tusks. The smile was a little panicked, a little hesitant, like he was afraid of me and what I might do—and really, could I blame him? But then it occurred to me, with a surge of panic, that he might look nervous because he'd figured out that I was a witch. Could orcs sense magic? Could he smell the witchcraft clinging to my skin like firesmoke?

As quickly as the wave of fear rose, it crashed back into the surf. No, that wasn't what I sensed from him. I wasn't as good at tasting the emotions of others as Brekka, but I was skilled enough to tell that there was no disgust or ill-will here. I borrowed power from Lena, sipping at the well of her animal aether to better suss out what it was I was getting from Orn. There was anxiety, self-consciousness, a protectiveness that made me melt, and—

Oh. Oh *my.*

I found desire lurking under it all, so intense and desperate it almost took my breath away. How was he hiding it so well? Just feeling it secondhand had me reeling, but without my magic I would never have known, he was so composed.

"Sleep well?" he asked, his voice breaking, making him flush, and in a flash I realized that there was an answering throb of want in me. I should have been too distracted and heartbroken to even notice Orn, let alone want him like this, but as soon as I gave that feeling attention it swelled and bubbled to the surface.

I nodded. "Very well!" I chirped, stretching and luxuriating in how his dark eyes tracked my movements. I couldn't seem to stop myself from preening, Lena "helping" by draping herself around my throat like a necklace, drawing the eye to my ample bosom, tragically hidden under the layers of baggy clothes I was borrowing. My stomach gave a loud gurgle, and I snapped out of my horny daydreaming and remembered that I had other needs that required attention beyond the ache that had started up between my legs. "What smells so good?" I asked, my voice breathy.

Orn scrambled to his feet, the huge orc making me a plate heaped high with food in the blink of an eye and holding it out to me. "Breakfast," he rumbled, letting me take the heavy plate —more a platter, really, in my much smaller hands—and then handing me a napkin and a spoon to eat with.

"Did you make all this for me?" I asked, incredulous, knowing I'd never be able to eat even a fraction of what he'd just given me. I'd never had a man feed me before, not like this, and somehow that only made me feel even more hot and bothered about him.

Naughty mama, Lena added, humor woven through her words.

"Uh...no?" His deep voice cracked again and he cleared his throat. "No, I made it for both of us. Is that enough?" He stood again, going to his cupboards and digging through them. "I can make more. I have a few potatoes for hash, and some more bread—"

I laughed, almost dropping my plate into my lap. "Gods, *no,* please don't cook any more!" He froze, staring at me as I laughed. "If I even finish *this* it'll be a miracle!" I explained.

He grinned sheepishly, biting his lip, and I finally managed to settle down and sober up a little. "I don't know how I'll ever thank you for all that you've done, Orn," I told him, wishing I were better with words. "You saved my life last night. And you've been so kind and generous without knowing me at all." I didn't say it, but he was nothing like how I'd always imagined orcs. The picture painted in my head was gruffer, more blunt and rude and bawdy, but Orn was just...sweet. Gentle. Something in me wanted to protect him, for all that he was close to seven feet tall and must have weighed over two hundred pounds, most of it rippling muscle.

I realized with a flare of shame that I'd unwittingly done to Orcish people what so many others had done to witches. I'd taken story and gossip as fact, when reality was bound to be different. Much like the gulf between stories about witches and the real thing. I resolved to do better.

He shrugged, blushing harder. "It was nothing," he insisted, retaking his seat and poking at his food. "Anyone would have done it."

But he was wrong; most people *wouldn't* have. They'd have given me water and a crust of bread, perhaps, and maybe let me shelter in their barn, but Orn had given me clothes, and home-cooked food, and his own bed. I eyed his aerlanis, up and chewing on something in a corner, and I was swept up in how kind of a heart wouldn't even let his *barn animal* wait out a storm in the barn. I swallowed hard, a lump in my throat, as I considered just how much the gods had smiled on me to lead me here last night.

I was struck by a mad urge to get up and subject Orn to a big hug. To throw my arms around his thick neck and squeeze him until my arms gave out, just because he was so damned *good*. But he was already tense just from my thanks, so I tamped that down and contented myself with digging into the food.

Flavor like I'd never encountered before burst on my tongue with my first bite of egg, and I couldn't stop myself from moaning like a shameless wanton at how incredible it was.

"What did you *do* to these eggs?" I cried, quickly shoveling in more. "These are the most delicious things I've ever eaten!"

Orn looked pleased and panicked at the same time, biting his lip again in an adorable gesture I was coming to love, despite how odd it looked with his tusks. "It's just more Orcish spice. You liked the tea last night, so I thought you might enjoy it."

I nodded enthusiastically, my mouth too full to speak for long minutes. "Damn right, I do," I told him. I gave him a sly look, licking salt and butter and spice from my lips as I held eye contact. "You better watch yourself, Orn; I might just have to tie you up and take you hostage to keep this incredible food coming." I liked to eat, but more than that, I liked Orn—and there was a part of me, the part not still ragged and aching from my recent loss—that really *really* liked Orn. It felt like a betrayal, to want something base and carnal when my coven—my *family* —had been torn away from me so recently, but the desire was there, and it was making itself known.

I eyed Orn, imagining what such big, gentle hands would feel like rasping over my skin. He had claws, though they weren't overlong, and I couldn't help but imagine them scraping into my flesh, dragging against my scalp. And then I was picturing darker, more explicit things. I stopped eating, my mind locking up imagining how Orn would make love to me. Would he be painfully gentle, treating me like delicate glass? Would he see to my pleasure before his own? Something told me yes, he would, and he'd push my body to its limits to do it. He'd make me scream and shudder and seep with orgasm after orgasm. And I thought, my heart stuttering and heat flooding my throbbing sex, that if I asked him nicely to fuck me hard and rough, that he'd do that, too.

I squirmed in my seat, throwing off blankets that had gotten too hot and rough against my sensitive flesh, the wetness between my thighs both winding me up and disturbing me at the same time. What was *wrong* with me, that I was so ready to lech on the kind stranger who'd helped me in my hour of need?

He was probably not even truly interested in me; I was human, and very different from the Orcish women he'd be used to. I was soft, plush, and while I knew I was beautiful, who was to say that an orc would see the same beauty? I busied myself with eating, doing my best to banish my heated thoughts and focus on the here and now.

I raised my gaze from my plate, unable to resist glancing at Orn, and to my surprise, he was staring at me, an expression on his flushed face like amazement. His hands were clamped tight on the edge of the table, claws digging into the wood, veins and tendons standing out stark against his warm green skin everywhere I could see. I was alarmed, my plate lowering to my lap. "Orn? Are you alright?" I asked, cold dread winding into my stomach and souring my meal.

He pushed back from the table and strode to the door in a rush, his frame tense and his back kept carefully to me. "I've just realized I need more wood for the fire!" he called over his shoulder, throwing a coat, scarf, boots, and a pair of gloves on at the door. "I'll be a little while, so go ahead and finish eating and then feel free to poke about!" His voice was tight and ragged, and he cleared his throat a little before speaking again. He turned towards me a little more, enough that I could see his face in profile. "Lock the door behind me and don't open it for anyone, Sara. You'll know it's me because I'll knock like this—" he rapped on the wall, a short, quick rhythm: *dundundunDUN, dundundunDUN.*

"O...kay..." I said slowly, concerned and confused at the sudden shift in his demeanor. "If I did something to offend you, I'm truly sorry, Orn. I was just kidding about the kidnapping, I hope you know—"

"Of course! I'm fine, you've nothing to worry about!" he called with false levity, throwing open his heavy door and stepping out into the howling wind and snow. "Remember, lock the door!" he threw over his shoulder as he shut the door, leaving me alone and blinking at the solid wood planks. *What in the names of the gods was* that? I thought, setting my unfinished plate onto the stool by the bed and stroking Lena's sweet little snub nose. I got up and did as Orn had said, setting the lock on the big door.

Strange man, Lena thought at me, and I nodded. *Chin now please,* she added after a moment. I obliged with a grin, switching to scratching her chin and throat, her thoughts becoming a constant stream of contentment and further instructions for me on where to tickle and scratch.

I did my best to clean up breakfast, putting the uneaten food into the small icebox and bringing the dishes to the sink. I couldn't get the water to work, though, so I was forced to leave them there. I combed out my hair with my fingers, wincing at the endless knots in my long curls, then found a small lavatory and took care of my overfull bladder and my morning breath. The water in here, at least, seemed to work, so I also found a rag and cleaned my skin, keeping my clothes on to ward off the chill. It was much colder here, away from the fire, and the cold water didn't help anything.

Once I was freshened up, I wandered around the small, cozy cabin, admiring Orn's few possessions and looking for something to do while I waited for him to come back from fetching more wood. I felt guilty, like I was the reason he had to go out there, and with a stab of dismay I realized that I probably was—he'd had to build the fire up higher to take care of me, and used up more of his firewood in the process. I sighed, throwing myself back onto the bed.

There was an unexpected crinkle when my body met the mattress, and I sat up, brow lowered in confusion. I dug through the blankets until I found a sheaf of parchments, so well worn that my lying on them didn't seem to have caused any additional wrinkling. The pages were filled with cramped, spidery Common, and after a sentence or two, I realized I was reading a story—a very *explicit* story

Corella's creamy skin glowed pink from her exertions, her small, pointed breasts swaying and shivering with the force of the orc's hips slamming into her own. She mewled, small hands clawing into his arms and chest as the much larger orc captain pounded into her tight, wet slit.

Well, there goes the last of my self-control, I thought, my blood burning and humming in my veins.

I kept reading, my arousal heating into a wild blaze. It felt wrong, to read something that was clearly private. And there was the distinct possibility that Orn had written this himself— but even if he hadn't, the condition of it spoke to its being well-loved. *Bet that means I was right,* my horny self purred at the back of my mind. Orn probably *would* fuck me senseless.

Something about that man had me thinking with my pussy, and I mused that perhaps my threat to tie him up and keep him might not have been so idle, after all.

CHAPTER FIVE

Hardwood

ORN

I knew that I shouldn't have bolted like that, but I was left with no choice; when I caught the scent of Sara's arousal on the air, thick and tangy-sweet like honey, my body's reaction was immediate and violent. Between one breath and the next my cock was an aching bar thrusting up obscenely from my groin, straining for Sara like a dog begging for table scraps. I'd felt my whole body heat and swell, my pulse thundering in my ears like a battle song. It had been all I could do to stop myself from tossing the table into the wall and pouncing on her then and there, when she'd done nothing but eat her food quietly.

I hadn't pressed her for details, but it was obvious that the little human woman had been through something awful before she made her way to my cabin seeking shelter and aid. I was the worst kind of monster to lust after her while she was so vulnerable. *But she was aroused,* something dark and sinuous inside me whispered, nipping at my heels with questions. But it didn't matter how aroused she was, the rational part of me knew; sometimes the body reacted strangely to stress and upset. And if she wanted me, she'd surely say something. Or give any indication at all of her interest. But Sara had been nothing but sweet and polite.

Calm down, you lout, I told myself as I finally reached my tool shed and dug out a wedge of the drifted-up snow to let me pull the door open and slip inside. My chopping axe was on the back wall, I knew—though it was too dark and murky in here to see. But I paused instead of grabbing it, my gloved hand drifting towards my groin, where my arousal was still howling and insistent. I bit my lip, glancing at the door, before ripping my gloves off with a growl and dropping my loose pants to my ankles, freeing my throbbing cock from its confines. I sank to my knees, my hand already stroking the hot, leaking length before I'd even fully settled. Bliss radiated from even that small, rough touch, and I groaned, my eyes squeezing closed.

With the silence and the dark all around me, knowing that there was no chance Sara would stumble upon me or hear me, I let myself fall into a fantasy. I conjured her deep brown skin and large, lively eyes. I pictured her sinfully full lips, so plush it felt like they couldn't be real, parted around panting breaths. I imagined what her large, heavy breasts might look like as they bounced and swayed under me. I imagined it was her honeyed cunt clenching around my shaft, rather than my hand, that her soft skin was under my other hand instead of being braced against my own thigh.

"Sara," I ground out, utterly lost in the scene playing out behind my eyes, "You're so fucking beautiful. So soft. I need you. Give me everything."

Pleasure crested, my sac wrenching up tight and liquid heat barreling up my spine. I slowed my hand's desperate pace, dancing on the razor's edge before release for several blissful seconds, an undignified whine escaping from my lips. But even in my imagination, I had to ensure my partner came first, and so it wasn't until I conjured Sara bucking and screaming under me, her neck arched and taut and her eyes rolled up into her skull, that I let my fist slide down to my swollen, sensitive knot and squeeze it like it was lodged in her cunt.

I came with a shattered roar, my body falling forward and my vision going spotty from the force of my orgasm. I could hear my seed hissing and spattering against the cold dirt floor of the shed, each hard throb rocking me and threatening to tug me unconscious. It went on for long seconds, longer than any other in my life, and by the end of it I was weak and trembling, wrung out and half-dead.

Once my vision cleared and I could get a proper lungful of air, I rose on shaky legs, pulling my pants back up and over my hips, wincing at the rub of the fabric over my too-sensitive flesh. I grabbed the axe from the wall and opened the door again for some light so I could kick dirt onto the river of seed painted across the floor.

With a heaving sigh, I left the shed, turning to my woodcutting area. I chopped wood for close to an hour in the snow, letting the burn in my muscles and the sweat running down my body cleanse my spirit of the last of its unwelcome lusts. Sara was my *guest*, was trusting me to take care of her and protect her from whatever she'd been running from, and I would not, under any circumstances, abuse that trust.

Once I was thoroughly worn out and had a nice pile of fresh logs to bring inside, I returned my chopping axe to its place in the shed, eyeing the conspicuous dirt piles with shame, and bundled the wood to bring inside. I knocked on the front door in the pattern I'd showed Sara earlier, pleased she'd listened to me and locked it, and waited for her to open the door for me.

I wasn't waiting long, the latch clattering on the other side in an instant, but I wasn't prepared for what welcomed me when I helped her push the heavy ironwood door open.

The smell of arousal was stronger than ever, re-inflating my traitorous cock in an instant. The scent was so thick on the air I could taste it, was dazed by it like it had struck me in the head with the force of a boulder.

And clutched in her small brown hands was the story I'd

been reading in bed when she'd arrived last night, forgotten and no doubt trapped somewhere among the blankets for her to find. I cursed myself a thousand times, preparing to slam the door shut in her face and just *run*, but before I could she grabbed my coat lapels and dragged me inside with surprising strength, kicking the door shut behind us both.

CHAPTER SIX

Sara Discovers The Fictional Girls

<u>SARA</u>

Orn had been gone for a damned long time, and after reading the story I'd found in the blankets, I was so wound up and desperate for release I'd felt like I'd crawl up the walls if he didn't show up soon. Lena hissed and rolled all over herself in a literal ball of irritation, my mood overwhelming her tiny snaky mind.

I knew Orn was attracted to me. Even without using my magic to tell me so it was written in the way his eyes lingered on me and drank me in when he thought I wasn't paying attention. But even after only knowing him a few hours I could tell he was too sweet and shy to make the first move, and I'd have to be the one to initiate things. For once, that didn't bother me, might even have excited me further. I felt like, despite how physically overwhelming Orn was, that I'd have all the power, and it was heady.

Underneath the searing heat of my need was a tiny current of something else, something that needed to affirm that I was still alive. I needed to release the nerves and the tension that had been building in me ever since I had come back to an empty hamlet practically burned to the ground, and me and Orn were both adults. If he'd have me, then that was all that really mattered. I could have taken care of myself while he was gone, of course, but that hadn't seemed...satisfying.

I wanted to get fucked, and I wanted Orn to be the one to do it.

"I'm a witch, Orn," I told him as he staggered inside from the force of my grip on his coat, closing the door behind him and re-locking it. My breasts were heavy, aching things, my erect nipples rubbing against the fabric of my borrowed shirt with every heavy breath. "Does that bother you?"

He blinked at me, clutching his pile of chopped wood like a lifeline. "I...what?"

"Does it bother you that I'm a witch?"

His brow scrunched, but he shook his head. "Of course not. What's going on? What's wrong?"

I let my body drift closer to his, crowding him against the wall despite how he towered over me. "I want you, Orn. Do you want me?"

His dark eyes widened, locked on my face, and I saw his throat bob several times. I held my breath, hoping I hadn't ruined everything by doing this, but just when I was about to give into despair he nodded. I shoved the wood out of his hands, heedless of the loud mess it made. His aerlanis bleated and pawed at the ground in her corner, Lena leaving her perch on the bed at my silent command to curl up on the hearthstones.

The sound of the wood crashing to the floor hadn't even properly faded from the close, warm air of the cabin before I was hopping up and throwing my arms around his strong neck. I hauled myself up his thick, strong body until I could reach his mouth and kiss him. For one breath, then two, he was frozen against me, his arms going around my back as a reflex more than anything. But finally he melted, his head tilting to give me better access to his differently-shaped mouth.

There was no room for slowness or caution where I'd gone, my lips crashing against his and my tongue and teeth nipping and licking and biting until he opened for me, submitted to me, let me taste him. He was flavored with the spices from breakfast, but underneath that I tasted *him*, and it was warm and soft and sweet. I sank deeper into the kiss, wanting to drink him down and swallow him whole.

He groaned, his arms shifting around me to get a better grip and haul me closer. His hands settled on my ass, gripping the generous expanse of flesh. He squeezed me, shuddering, and I felt something prod at me that wasn't his hands—it must have been his cock, and the realization made me shiver.

Orn pushed off the wall, spinning us until it was me that was pinned in place, his hips coming forward to brace against mine to hold me up so his hands could roam. He didn't seem to know what he wanted to touch first, his hands cupping my face, sinking into my hair, slipping under my shirt to caress my round belly and sides. But he stayed away from where I wanted him most, and that simply would not do.

I wrapped my legs tight around his waist, anchoring myself in place, and used my arms to peel off my tunic and sweater, baring myself to him from the waist up. His eyes immediately locked onto my breasts, the peaks dark and hard and insistent. He bit his lip again, and I grinned, slinging my arms around his neck once more.

"Touch me, Orn." I rolled my hips, loving the way he gasped when my ass brushed against his blatant arousal. "Please. I need you to touch me."

He nodded, swallowing again, and then his head dipped, his large nose sinking into the valley between my tits to take a deep breath of my skin. He groaned, one hand coming up to cup and knead and heft one breast, his eyes lifting to watch my face. I moaned, arching my back and pressing myself more firmly into his hand, and then he was taking my nipple into his mouth, his jutting tusks bracketing the tight bud, and to my surprise I quite liked the sensation, that contrast between hard and soft. "Yes, Orn," I panted, my arms sliding up to cradle his head against me. "Just like that, honey."

He shuddered again, his cock bucking up into me from where it poked at my backside, and then he was straightening up, hefting me in his arms and carrying me over to the bed. He set me down gently, making sure my head landed on a pillow, before returning to my breasts with a mad vigor. I cried out, writhing under him, as he explored my body with a pent-up kind of energy that felt like a sheathed blade. I could *feel* him holding back, pacing himself, and a wicked part of me wanted to provoke him into losing that control. I was feeling daring and dangerous, desperate to sink into pleasure.

Just then, Orn lifted his head, his deep green lips gleaming and swollen. He lunged for my mouth again, stealing my breath with his heat. I arched up into him, my skin tingling and oh-so-sensitive where it brushed against his clothes.

Wait. He was still clothed? *That* wouldn't do.

I brought my hands up to blindly fumble over his clothing, seeking out buttons and ties and belts that I could undo, but unwilling to stop kissing him to do it. His mouth may have been strange to me, but it was a good kind of strange, full of promises for things that both thrilled and soothed me. He was the most attentive man I'd ever kissed, alternating between hard and hot and soft and sweet with an uncanny knack for what I wanted. At last my fingers found ties, and I wasted no time in undoing them, loosening his jacket enough to shove it off of his strong, broad shoulders. He helped me from there, taking it off the rest of the way, then breaking our kiss just long enough to peel off the sweater and tunic beneath it.

The olive green of his skin was stunning, the thick mat of black curls over his chest and trailing down his abdomen calling out for my fingers and my mouth. I couldn't help but notice how pretty we looked together, the deep brown of my own skin against his olive. Then he was lunging for me again, desperate hands kneading at my plushness, hefting me with growled-out appreciation that made me want to purr and preen.

His mouth left mine, trailing along my jaw with a feather-lightness that morphed once he got to my throat, growing hungry and insistent, almost...*claiming*. He nipped at the tender skin there, making me jolt and gasp and shiver. "Too much?" he asked, switching to nuzzling me with his nose.

I shook my head. "No. It's wonderful. Keep going." I cradled his head closer, tilting my own head back to offer my throat to him more fully. Up close, his tusks looked dangerous, all wicked curve and sharp points, but I knew he wouldn't hurt me. He was practically a stranger, but somehow I *knew*.

He dove back in with a moan, his clawed hands continuing to wander over my body, and while this was good, it was wonderful, I couldn't help feeling a little...frustrated. I wanted more, *needed* more, and he was going so *slow*. Perhaps at a different time I'd be luxuriating in this kind of attention, but my lust in this moment was too urgent, my body pleading for release.

"Orn," I gasped out, grabbing his hand on my hip and trying to shove it between my legs. "I need more," I whined when his hand stopped moving towards my aching pussy, all my attempts to keep him moving meeting a brick wall. *Gods, he's so strong*, I thought dimly.

Orn pulled back, his long black hair wild around his square face, the look on his flushed face so serious it bordered on grim. He studied my face, and I tried to plead with every inch of me for him to *move*, to go where I needed him. At last, he nodded, gathering his long hair into a knot at the crown of his head that emphasized his sharp features, making him so beautiful it stunned me.

Then he unlaced my pants and yanked them over my wide hips and down my legs, baring me completely to the chill air of his cabin. He stood, considering me lying naked on his bed, and his throat bobbed. "Sweet Delenaa, you're so beautiful," he said, his voice low and rough with desire. It was such a deep rumble I could almost feel it peppering my skin, and I shivered once again. I'd never been so affected by a lover before. I spread my legs, my hand brushing over my skin, trailing down to my throbbing, needy sex. I parted the curls on my mound, then my lower lips, to expose my clit to his rapt gaze. I teased it lightly, showing him what I liked and goading him in one fell swoop. I arched for him, putting on a show, tempting him into further action, since it seemed he was a little *too* content to simply admire me.

I was shocked and delighted when he stood and grabbed my ankles, yanking me to the edge of the bed, his eyes dark lights that bore into me as he loomed.

CHAPTER SEVEN

She Be Comin' Up On That Mountain With His Tongue...

ORN

This little witch was *trying* to make me lose myself, to push me into wildness. It was obvious in the way she'd touched herself, a challenge gleaming on her pretty face, the way she tried to muscle me into different directions. But I had been waiting so long for this moment—too long, really—to allow myself to be goaded. For all her fire, Sara was still soft, still sweet, and when I wanted my own turn at leading she gave it easily. I didn't have to battle with her, to wrench control away and fight to keep it; being with Sara was everything I'd been craving from my other Orcish partners in the past. So while it felt wrong to deny her, I was too far gone, too greedy; she would take *what* I gave her, *when* I gave it to her.

But I would make sure she liked it.

I pulled her to the edge of the bed and sank to my knees, throwing her legs over my shoulders as I settled between her plush thighs. The scent of her arousal hit me like a fist, and I was glad I was already on my knees so she wouldn't see how weak she made me. Orc women were built much the same here as human women, but the flesh was harder, tougher, requiring more force and stimulation to give them sufficient pleasure, and it had been something I'd always struggled to get comfortable with.

But Sara was human; it didn't feel like I had to flirt with breaking her to make her feel good. My lightest caresses were eliciting such wonderful reactions from her, and that felt right, felt good, like nothing had before now. Sara was the first human that I'd been intimate with, and I could tell already that I was hopelessly addicted to this.

I leaned in and nuzzled at her silky-soft skin, pressing kisses to her delectably plump thighs, to the crease where her legs meet her pelvis, then to the crisp curls decorating the slick rose-brown folds peeking from between her lower lips. She mewled and bucked, trying to goad me again, and I growled low, unfurling my tongue from my mouth and licking a slow stripe up the seam of her. I knew it wasn't what she wanted, and I knew exactly where she *did* want me, but I wouldn't be rushed; I was having a *moment*.

I kissed and nipped and nuzzled, I drank in the scent of her skin and the deeper tangy-sweet musk of her sex, using my arms to pin her hips to the bed so that she could not help but be at my mercy, to let me enjoy myself.

"Orn," she whined, and something about her tone snapped my resolve to savor her. I paused, lifting my head to look up at her. She'd propped herself up on her elbows and was glaring down at me.

I couldn't help it; I grinned up at her, holding her tawny eyes as I lowered my mouth again and used my long tongue to lap at the swollen bud of her clit with a firm, twisting stroke.

She gasped and collapsed onto her back again, her hips straining against my grasp, wanting to press her tender flesh more firmly into my mouth. But I was nervous about my tusks so close to such delicate skin. So I kept her where I had her, paying close attention to what touches made her buck and gasp and writhe like she was losing her mind.

It wasn't long before I was lost in my task, my world reduced to her smell, her taste, her noises, and the carnal push and pull of figuring out what, exactly, she liked best. I was only dimly aware that she was crying out now, her fingers buried in my hair and tugging at it, sending little sparks of pain here and there on my scalp and undoing my careless bun. I paid more attention when she suddenly grew quiet, her whole body quivering and slick with sweat, and her nub throbbing against my tongue. Then she arched her back and keened, and a deluge of wetness coated my lower face, her sex clenching and throbbing against me.

I beamed, full of pride; I had made her come.

I gentled my movements, knowing that she would likely be too sensitive for several moments. But I didn't let up, chasing her moans and her cries, winding her back up until she was taut and ready to snap once more. Then I latched onto her thick bud, letting my tusks bracket her sex, and sucked on her.

This time when she came, it sounded like she was dying, her tight grip on my hair pulling several strands free from my scalp. But I was too concerned by the noises she made to linger on my own pain. The orgasm seemed to drag out for longer, causing her to spasm harder, and I worried for a moment that I'd been too forceful, that I had hurt her. I released her, springing to my feet and bending over her, cupping her sweet heart-shaped face in my hand and searching for signs of injury.

"Are you alright, Sara?" I asked, brushing errant curls back from her face. Her dazed eyes slid over my face, disturbingly blank, and I cursed myself for being so greedy.

"Wuh?" she asked, her brows furrowing.

"Are you alright?"

She blinked up at me, then surprised me utterly by laughing. She laughed long and loud, tears gathering on her lashes. She struggled to breathe around the sound erupting from her. "Am I *alright*?" she guffawed, patting my cheek with one of her tiny hands. "Honey, you just about sucked my soul out of my pussy, and I am *not* upset about that in the least."

I felt pride that I'd managed to please her so well on our first coupling. Something warm and glowing filled me when she called me 'honey', and though I knew she couldn't possibly mean anything by it, I found myself wishing she did.

I loosed a breath in relief, my hands skating over her face and neck, unable to stop myself from touching her. "So you are well?"

"Very," she purred, lifting up onto her elbows to kiss me again. "That was amazing."

She let herself drop onto her back, carding her fingers through my thick carpet of chest hair, tracing it down to where it thinned and trailed into my pants, where my cock was aching and leaking, desperate for her. She palmed it, and I hissed, my eyes rolling closed. I could not help but grind into her hand a little, seeking her warmth even though it had been very little time since I'd spilled my seed by my own hand. I hadn't been this wound up and sensitive since my teenage years.

"Let's take care of *you*, now, honey," she said, stroking me through the rough fabric. "I want you inside me, Orn."

I froze, fear jolting through me. I did not know if I was ready for that, after all. I was so much larger than her, my cock proportioned to fit into a much larger Orcish body. Her flesh was pliant, but would it be able to take me without injury? I thought that I would die if I hurt Sara, even on accident.

"I-I don't know if...if we'll fit," I admitted, carefully stroking through her folds, mindful of my claws. I pressed the pads of two of my fingers at her entrance, but it was hard to tell anything beyond that she was hot and soaked for me.

I stood, striding over to my kitchen and digging through a drawer until I found my good shears. I cut my claws down on my right hand, my dominant hand, making sure there were no sharp edges left before returning to Sara, who was watching me quizzically.

"What're you doing that for?" she asked, letting me help her back up the bed to rest against the pillows. "Are *you* well?"

I traced my newly-shorn finger through her folds, gathering her slick, and then I breached her, slowly, carefully, testing. Her cunt clenched on my finger, sucking it deeper into her body, and Sara grinned fiercely up at me. She relaxed into the pillow and spread her legs wider, beckoning me with her eyes, and I pulled my finger out to insert a second, eliciting a gasp from her. But she didn't look as though she was hurting, so I continued to stroke her inner walls, seeking out what felt good, and trying to determine if another finger would hurt her; my cock was certainly thicker than just two of my fingers.

I grazed a spot on the top of her channel that felt different from the rest, a little rougher, and she groaned, wiggling her hips to coax me to apply more pressure. "Sweet Delenaa, Orn," she cried out, her eyes rolling, "Yes! Oh, sweetness, *right there.*"

I did as she bid, stroking into that spot and trying not to linger too long on the things she was calling me. *It doesn't mean anything. It can't,* I told myself. I felt her begin to flutter and tighten around my fingers, her cunt hot and wet and welcoming, and I paused in my attentions just long enough to slip a third finger into her.

"Is that too much?" I asked, holding still. She shook her head, rolling her hips, and I resumed my movements, trying to stretch her carefully even as I stroked this special spot inside her and tried to make her climax once more.

She panted and shivered, her hands clinging tight to my forearms, her blunt little nails leaving half-moon indents in my skin, nonsense babbling from her sensual mouth. An idea struck me, and I used my other hand to roll her clit between two of my knuckles, trying to mimic what my mouth was doing to her not long ago. Her eyes snapped open and snagged mine, a look almost like betrayal crossing her features, and then she was screeching and writhing, her cunt clamping hard around my digits and her whole body shuddering and jolting with the force of her orgasm. She leaked copiously around my fingers, still buried inside her and stroking at that spot, as she continued to come and come and come. I didn't let up until she shoved me away, a look of stunned disbelief plastered on her flushed and sweaty face.

"I didn't know that was something I could do," she murmured, dazed. I licked my fingers clean, satisfied to have brought her such pleasure, and thinking perhaps she might be able to take my cock after all, if she really wanted it.

I got up to get her a glass of water, helping her sit up to drink it and catch her breath. In all honesty, I did not mind if she had changed her mind about taking me inside her; my cock ached fiercely, but moreso I ached with pride for being able to make her feel so good. I would happily explore her body more, spend the rest of the storm figuring out what touches brought her to the highest heights, that left her this glowing and boneless, without my cock ever leaving my pants.

But once she had finished her water she turned to me with a predatory glint in her eye, and before I knew it she had her hands on my pants and was tearing them loose from my body. A seam audibly ripped as she tugged and yanked. I laughed, helping her get them off of me, and then we were both naked in my bed.

CHAPTER EIGHT

The Dam Breaks

<u>**SARA**</u>

To say that that had been the best orgasm of my life almost cheapened it, reduced it to a thing that was "just"—just an orgasm, just a bodily reaction. But it had felt cosmic and huge, like something had shaken loose while my body throbbed and pulsed and broke into stars over and over again.

And now I was staring at his cock, and it was just as big and beautiful as the rest of him. It was textured in ways I never could have anticipated, my experience thus far exclusively with humans, but I wasn't afraid of it. That would require my being afraid of Orn, and despite only knowing him for less than a day, that already felt impossible.

I licked my lips, reaching for him, but I paused to ask, "Can I touch you?"

He nodded, face flushed and throat bobbing. He held himself stiff and tense in his seat at the edge of the bed, as if he was worried I was going to spook and run if he made the wrong move, and it was so sweet yet sad I couldn't help but crawl into his lap. I slung one arm around his neck and slid the other slowly down his body, over his heaving chest and trembling belly, until I had an overflowing fistful of orc cock. I gave him a squeeze, making him gasp, and I swallowed the soft sound with a kiss.

It was a sweeter kiss, less wild than they'd been so far, and I found myself sinking into it like I'd sunk into his soft, warm bed after my endless march through the blizzard. He felt right in a way I couldn't quite pin down, and it wasn't just because the complex bumps and ridges of his cock in my hand had me feeling aching and wanton in anticipation.

My arm around his neck tightened, pressing us closer together, and even though he was so much larger and stronger than me, he came easily, gladly, his hands grabbing me and clutching me tight. I felt bright, I felt wanted, but I also felt empty and aching. I wanted to taste Orn, but I thought it would have to wait for another time, because I was beginning to feel overwhelmed with the desire for him to fill me.

I shifted, sitting higher, breaking our kiss to do so, and used my grip on his shaft to guide it to the swollen, sensitive core of me, shuddering just from the press of his fat, blunt head at my entrance. Before I could ask him if he was okay with what I was doing, he spoke, his dark eyes wild on mine. "Yes, Sara," he rasped, his fingers digging into my hips, claws *just* pricking at the skin of my ass. "Ride me, please."

I started to sink down onto him, and he tipped his head back, something between a growl and a whine ripping from his throat. "Please," I heard him whisper, and it grabbed at me and wrenched something loose in my chest. Emotion swelled, and when tears threatened with a tight ache in my throat I slammed myself down onto him, gasping and crying out at the sensation. He was so big, so thick, and with all the added texture it almost felt like an invasion. But he held me tenderly, kissing my neck and chest, his hands unsteady but caressing me gently. He murmured how good I felt, how proud he was that I'd taken all of him, and my emotions began to settle. After a few deep breaths, the sting faded and I rolled my hips, testing.

We both moaned, our combined fluids making obscene sounds as I slowly started to ride him, the last of the tension from the pain fading as I opened myself to the sensations, to what it felt like to be surrounded by Orn, filled by him, utterly tangled together with him. He kept his hips still, letting me lead, his focus on worshiping everything he could reach of my body with that tender sweetness that I was coming to realize he was overflowing with. It made me wonder what he could have possibly done to wind up all alone and so far from home. Maybe he was up here in the mountains for the same reason that I was; because there was nowhere else in the world that he fit into. But unlike me, he hadn't found a family of people like him waiting for him in these mountains.

I began to ride him faster, my legs burning from so much activity over the last few days, but I couldn't stop—I could feel another orgasm building, this one deep and languorous, a heated coil gradually winding through my body. My eyes were closed, my concentration going towards chasing that feeling, to sinking into it as deeply as I could.

So I didn't see how one of Orn's hands dipped down between my legs. But I sure felt it when careful fingers found my clit, just resting on it and letting the jostle of our bodies do all the moving.

I cried out, pleasure mounting hard and fast now, but just then my left leg locked up, and I froze, my eyes snapping open with a wince. "Cramp," I bit out, going to rub it loose before I lost this feeling.

But before I knew it I was tipping back, Orn's hand cradling the back of my head, making sure I wound up exactly where he wanted me. He guided my cramped up leg out straight and used two knuckles to massage my knotted thigh muscle. But he didn't stop fucking me, his strokes long and smooth and maddeningly slow, keeping my arousal peaked but my orgasm just out of reach.

"You've been through a lot," he told me, his gaze hot and

firm as he loomed over me. "Let me take care of you, sweetheart." I shuddered at the epitaph, his tenderness swamping me and stealing my voice. But I managed a nod, my hands coming up to stroke along his jaw and clasp his strong shoulders. *Please take care of me*, I tried to say with my eyes. *Make me feel good.*

He dipped his head to kiss me, the hard press of his tusks no longer odd but welcome. He peppered my face with soft kisses, his length still sliding in and out of me, winding me up, and I sighed and rolled my hips up into his, trying to coax him into moving faster. My leg was mostly back to normal now, and I wanted *more*. I wanted it all, every inch and drop of him.

He noticed my squirming and paused. "Are you alright?"

I nodded, then bit my lip. "My leg feels fine now. I need more, Orn."

His dark eyes searched my face, his body going tense under my hands, and I couldn't help but huff in frustration. "You won't break me," I promised him, hooking my legs around his waist and letting my nails dig into his back as I used my heels to press him harder into me. "Can you give me what I want?" I taunted, arching my eyebrow and tipping my chin up defiantly.

He frowned, his long hair curtaining us and making his features more stark and sharp with shadow. But I wasn't afraid, even though he looked fearsome. He was my big, sweet orc savior, he was Orn, and even if he let loose I had no doubt that I was safer with him than I'd ever been with anyone else.

Without warning, he was slamming into me, hitting something deep inside of my pussy, his lips twisting in a snarl that felt feral. "You want more?" he growled, beginning an unforgiving rhythm that had my eyes rolling and my limbs curling in like a dead bug. "You'll get it. You'll get anything you want, sweetheart. Just say the word."

My awareness bled and faded, bliss pulsing out from my core and coating every nerve in my body like a sweet sticky syrup. I was making wild noises, sounds I never suspected I could make, but Orn was taking me just how I'd wanted, and it was better than any fantasy could have conjured. There was no room left in me to care about how I looked or sounded. I never wanted it to end, I wanted to stay in this crystalline moment of pleasure for the rest of my life, where fear for the future was distant and remote, where I was cared for and safe and warm.

But he felt so good, too good, and I was coming yet again with a howl, my throat shredding itself raw as I screamed my pleasure, thanking the gods who'd delivered me here.

It felt like I was flying, my spirit free of my body and tasting the heavens, but there were thick arms cradling me, warm work-roughened hands stroking my skin, combing my curls back from my sweat-sticky face, and a deep, rough voice was calling to me.

I blinked a few times, my vision clearing of stars, and Orn's handsome face swam into focus, fear and concern hewn into his features. "Are you alright?" he asked, panic in his voice. "Did I hurt you?"

I laughed, an embarrassing sound like a braying donkey. "No, honey," I managed after a moment, tucking a lock of his dark hair behind a pointed green ear. "You did *very* well."

His lips quirked up in a small smile. "I thought I might have done something wrong. You sounded like a banshee on the moors."

I laughed again, the sound more normal this time. "No, no, no—that's how you know you've done everything *right*." I pulled him down, urging him to put more of his weight on me, because it felt amazing, and it helped ground me. "You're amazing, Orn," I whispered into his ear, and beneath the boneless satiation making me feel heavy and loose something sparked. "You fucked me so good, honey," I purred, stroking up and down the long, firm line of his spine. "Now I want *you* to come. I want you to give me everything you have. Will you do that for me?"

His cock bucked inside me, his big body shuddering against

mine. His head fell into the crook of my neck, his proud nose taking in big lungfuls of my scent. He started to move again, and I heard only one word from him, a soft sigh: "Yes."

It felt like I shouldn't be able to come again, not so many times in a row, not after such an earth-shattering one, but the desperate, needy rhythm of Orn's hips had something dredging itself up from the depths of me to try anyway. I gasped and moaned and panted in his ear, letting him know how good he felt, how well he was doing, because it felt right, to pepper such a tender man with tender words. His hands grasped my hips, guiding them into a new angle, and my vision blinked out for a moment, his thick, textured cock hitting something new and overwhelming the synapses in my brain.

He started to moan in my ear, the sound too sexy for words, and then his pace stuttered and grew uneven, and then he was slamming into me *hard*, something even thicker but blessedly smooth forcing its way into me, tearing a gasp from me. It burned, the stretch almost too much, but then he was shuddering and gasping and whimpering, holding me tight as hot seed bathed my insides. The heat soothed away the sting, allowing me to feel the steady throb as this new part of him inside me did whatever it did.

Whatever it was, it was hitting the sweet spot near my entrance *just* right, wringing another orgasm from my exhausted body. It was weaker, more brief, but it felt good anyway, and I sank into the bed beneath me with a sigh.

Orn was still shuddering above me, his breaths ragged. His cock was still bucking, still emptying into me, though it felt like it had at least slowed down. It was going to be a huge mess when we parted.

It was going to be a huge mess when we parted.

Something about that thought *hurt*, dug into my tender parts like a thorn. When Orn started to nuzzle and hold me, shifting us onto our sides with sweet care, everything that I'd been holding back surged up, crested into a wave I had no choice but to drown under, and before I knew it I was weeping.

CHAPTER NINE

A Thrall Is Born

ORN

Being with Sara had done something to me that felt like magic, and I wondered idly if this is why she'd felt the need to tell me that she was a witch. Had she cast a spell on me? Stolen my soul? Bound me to her service as a thrall?

I decided immediately that none of that mattered, none of it bothered me, and I'd be happy to follow her to the ends of the earth as her devout meat puppet, so long as she kept looking at me like she did. So long as she kept calling me "honey".

She was shuddering in my arms now, her body so soft and warm and right, and even if stars were still dancing before my eyes and my heart felt like it was trying to pound its way out of my chest, I couldn't help but think this was the happiest I'd ever been in my life. This sweetness, this tenderness was what was missing from my couplings with other orcs. Even if I missed my family, this convinced me more than anything else that leaving had been a good decision. Painful and awful in many ways, but *correct*.

My mind was scattered like so many dandelion seeds on the wind, so it took longer than I liked to admit to realize that something was wrong. Sara wasn't just shuddering from aftershocks, and the warm liquid dripping onto the bicep she was using as a pillow wasn't sweat. Her snake pet Lena—or perhaps she was actually Sara's familiar—slithered her way onto the bed and piled herself onto the exposed side of Sara's head in a loose, messy pile. I froze, the afterglow shattering and raw, screaming panic sending adrenaline surging through me.

Sara was crying.

My cock was rapidly softening at the realization, but my knot deflated on its own time, and though I wanted to yank myself free and run from the horror of what I'd done, I was trapped.

"What have I done?" I asked, trying to pull back from her, to give her what space I could. "I hurt you."

But Sara clung to me, a shaky "no" slipping between the heart-wrenching sobs that she was making freely now. Lena blinked up at me, tasting the air with her little tongue, and I could almost swear she was trying to tell me something, that there was some reassurance in her tiny black eyes. All I could do was lie there, holding Sara and trying to soothe her, my brain locked up and most of me frozen as I struggled to understand what had happened and where it had all gone wrong. The only reason I didn't utterly lose my mind was Sara clinging to me, holding me tight, and even if half of me was screaming that I'd done something bad, something wrong, the other half was insisting that she wouldn't do that if she feared or hated me.

"What's wrong, sweetheart?" I kept asking her, "What happened? Did I hurt you?" But it was long moments before she was calm enough to answer me. Lena still twined through her hair and over her ear, occasionally dipping lower to brush over an eyebrow or a damp eye. A few times the little hognose even nuzzled at my chest, where Sara now hid her lovely face.

Once Sara quieted, she went so still and silent that I thought at first that she had fallen asleep. But then she took a deep, shuddering breath and spoke into my chest, her voice so rough it hurt to hear it. "You didn't do anything wrong, honey. I'm...I'm sorry."

That eased some of the tension in my body, but now I was worried about what else could possibly be wrong that would make this woman—so strong and steadfast and bold—collapse like this. "What's wrong? What can I do to help?"

She pulled back enough to swipe at her face with one of her delicate little human hands, grimacing at what she wiped away. "Can you get me a handkerchief? Or a rag? And some water would be lovely, too."

I eased my hips back, making sure my knot was as deflated as it felt, and when I slipped free from her hot, silky cunt I mourned the loss, but I was glad I could fetch her what she needed. I gathered rags first, stuffing a handful between her legs to catch our spend and handing her another softer one for her face. Then I rushed to my sink, pumping water into a glass for her to drink and using more to dampen yet another rag to clean her up with. I used a corner on myself, sucking in a breath at the cold, wet fabric on my sensitive skin, and then held it near the fire for a moment to try to warm it. Once it was no longer frigid, I returned to her, helping her sit up to drink the water and carefully wiping her gleaming brown skin clean with the damp rag. Lena re-situated herself into a clumsy sort of hat, and Sara reached up to stroke her little friend. It didn't take long for Sara to finish the water, and I took the empty glass and refilled it, setting it nearby for her, and also took the soiled rags and tossed them aside.

Then I decided she also needed food, so I sprang back to my feet to dug through my icebox until I found the last piece of the apple cake I'd made before the storm hit, setting it on my cast iron pan and letting it heat over the fire while I poured a measure of mead into a cup and handed it to her.

Sara sipped at the mead, her eyes downcast and hollow, and I added a piece of brown bread slathered with my precious honey butter to the plate I put the warm apple cake on, as well as some smoked cheese and nuts. The more I looked at her sorrowful expression, the more I wanted to add to the plate, but I recalled how little she had been able to eat of breakfast, and forced myself to stop after that. I handed her the plate, sitting beside her on the bed, but too scared to touch her.

She took the plate, blinking in surprise, then chuckled, a broken smile slipping through the clouds to light her face. "Thank you, Orn," she croaked, pinching a chestnut between her fingers and bringing it to her lips. She set the plate in her lap, reaching up to lift her snake up and off of her head and draping her around her neck instead. "And you *know* you're not supposed to sit there, young lady," she told Lena sternly. Lena's tiny head rocked a little, and I could have sworn that that was a serpentine shrug of some sort.

Sara picked at her food, tasting no more than a bite of any one thing, and eventually gave up, setting it aside beside her water glass. She scooted closer to me, tugging on my arm until I realized she was trying to coax me closer. I moved to sit with my back resting against the headboard, and she dove into me, slipping under my arm and resting her head on my chest. Her arms wrapped around my waist, and she sighed, tugging the blankets up around herself until they were tucked under her chin.

"The things that happened before I came here were very bad," she whispered, and I tightened my grip on her. "It was my turn, so I was out foraging for reagents, and when I came back, everyone was gone. Taken. *All* of them, all my sisters and my mothers. My entire coven, just—" she ended on a sob, the words choked off, and I felt foolish and useless in the face of her grief. I was banished and knew what it was to lose all of your family in one fell swoop, but knowing that they still lived and could find happiness and love even if I wasn't there to share in it had been something of a comfort to me. It sounded as though Sara had no idea where they were, what had happened to them, or whether they were even still alive, and I could not begin to process how lost and unmoored she must have felt.

"I'm so sorry," I told her, knowing my words were small and pathetic. But she squeezed me and gave me her thanks anyway. I panicked quietly as I struggled to think of what to say, wanting to know more but also wanting to respect her privacy and not dredge up anything worse than I had already.

In the face of her grief, something began to stir in me, something that I couldn't say I'd really ever felt before. It growled and seethed, coursing through my limbs and making them feel restless. It needed something, this feeling, and I was afraid to focus on it because it reeked of copper.

Once she composed herself, she went on, her voice flat, I suspected in an attempt to keep the emotion from overwhelming her again. I hoped she knew she didn't have to tell me any of this, that I didn't expect it, but I didn't want to interrupt her to tell her. "I don't know who did it, but there's those in the village below that fear and hate witches and resent our presence here. There've been attempts in the past to try and get us to leave, but these mountains belong to no one, so they couldn't exactly evict us." She lapsed into silence, sniffling and burrowing closer. "I just wish I knew what happened," she continued eventually, her voice small and soft. "If they're—if they're okay, if they're still alive. Gods, it's like I'm missing a huge chunk of myself. A coven is such a sacred thing."

The smell of copper was joined by a wild drumbeat thundering through my head, my veins, beating against the inside of my ribs. I'd begun to grind my teeth, tusks catching my upper lip and gouging into it hard enough to hurt. What was this? What was going on with me that I felt like this? I'd been angry before, but not like this. Nothing had ever been like this.

Sara squeezed me and seemed to realize just how tense and quiet I'd gone. She tilted her head back, looking up into my face, and even though I tried to hide my face behind my long black hair, she must have caught sight of my expression anyway. She sat up, her hands stroking my skin in soft, soothing motions that should have been calming me down. But for some reason, her sweetness only stoked the fire in my veins hotter and higher.

"Orn? What's wrong? Are you okay?" She bit her lower lip, her brows coming together in concern. "Was all that too much? I'm sorry, I should have asked before laying that all on you—"

"No," I ground out, horrified that she thought she'd done something wrong. I took a deep breath, trying to will myself calm, but the tension remained, the...the *bloodlust*. In a flash, I knew what this was—for the first time in my life, I felt the blood song, birthright of every orc, that had never so much as murmured through me before. I grabbed her face and tugged her close, wanting to smash my mouth to hers and claim her again, my cock already awakening despite being thoroughly drained twice today already. But I paused before my lips made it to hers. "Can I kiss you?" I asked, my voice a rough stranger in my ears.

In answer she closed the distance left between us, her mouth hesitant on mine for a moment, but she did bloom, and *gods* what a blooming she was. She was all that was good and sweet in this world. I knew it with a perfect clarity that defied our status as barely more than strangers. And then it clicked, the blood song finally taking on words I could hear and understand.

I tried to sear myself into her skin, devouring her even as I fed her all I had, wanting to mark her in a primal way that it took every ounce of willpower to ignore. It became a goodbye, because I knew that even though the thought was agony, I would be leaving her.

My body ached for something she couldn't give me. It howled for blood, for the blood of those who had hurt her by stealing her family. It was a need greater than any I had ever felt before, more keen than the sharpest hunger, deeper than the worst thirst. I knew from my people's stories that unless I pursued the song my body would sicken, my mind unraveling, until I couldn't help but give it what it wanted. It was why my people were generally feared and thought of as brutal; small minds always saw what they wanted, mistaking my peoples' gift as a thing of pure violence. But the blood song had kept us safe when outsiders had tried to wipe us out to take what was ours. It had made it so that generations of orcs across Cillure— from the Orcish of the Fenns to the Jeargan of the Isles—were powerful enough to keep the clans intact, to keep our roots strong. The blood song was often violent, yes—but it was not a violence *we* had created the need for.

The blood song in its purest form was a shield to protect. And now that it throbbed through me, I could see with cold-sharp clarity that Sara needed that shield. The people who'd hurt my little witch would pay for their crimes. And *I* would be the one to make sure that debt was collected.

CHAPTER TEN
Blood Song

<u>SARA</u>

Orn was scaring me, a murderous rage flaring along every line of his body that only eased when he looked at me. It made my chest do strange swooping things that were entirely inappropriate right now.

Big angry, Lena said, watching Orn from my shoulder. *Why leave? Snuggles good.* I smiled sadly, scratching her chin.

"I don't know," I whispered, watching Orn pace and fume, occasionally grabbing an item of clothing and just about shredding it in his big clawed hands. Those hands had been so gentle and delicious on my body not all that long ago, but now I could see how they might moonlight as a murder weapon.

"Orn," I called again, trying for perhaps the dozenth time to get an explanation from him, "what's going on? Are you leaving?"

This time he paused, my words finally reaching him. "Aye, I'm leaving," he said, his Fenns accent stronger than I'd heard it yet. "I've important things to do, my sweet one."

I ignored the pleased glow that settled in my belly at his tenderness, lifting my chin and squaring my shoulders, trying to look stern despite being utterly naked outside of the clumsy snake adorning my neck and shoulders. "I don't *want* you to leave, though." I glanced at the nearest window. While the storm was beginning to calm, it was certainly far from safe for traveling. Orn couldn't go out in that, no matter how important what he was trying to do. "It's not safe. And I...I'd rather not be alone right now. I—I want you to stay close." I lowered my eyes, just for a minute, hating how bare I felt, but I re-firmed myself a moment later; he needed to know I meant it.

Orn groaned, tossing aside the belt he'd been trying his best to strangle, and going to his knees at the bedside. He reached for me, cradling my face carefully. "I know now's not a good time, but there's no reasoning with it, sweetheart. It's either give it what it wants or risk going berserk...and doing what it wants, anyway. Gods know my words to be true: I don't *want* to leave. But the song..."

Something tickled at my memory, something whispered about orcs, but that I'd never been sure was real. "The blood song?" I asked, hoping the question wasn't rude.

He nodded, his handsome face tense and his neck a stark road map of tendons and veins, like he was holding back something massive. "I don't know what I'll do if I don't tend to it. It's never come on before, not for me. Can you understand that?"

I nodded. "What is it that you need to do?"

His fury morphed into sheepishness, his thumbs stroking my cheeks. "It's uh...well..."

I arched an eyebrow. "What is it?" I deadpanned, my hands coming up to rest over his, still cupping my face. I squeezed what I could of his huge mitts, looking up into his dark eyes. "Tell me, Orn."

"It's just...I-have-to-find-your-coven-for-you-and-murder-whoever-took-them-and-made-you-sad," he finally spat out in a breathless rush.

I considered that. It made me uncomfortable to take still

64

more help from him, to impose on him yet again when I'd already done so much of it, but I wasn't actually asking for this. Strictly speaking, he wasn't even *offering* to help me in this way; he was just telling me that he was going to do it no matter what. And there was no denying that having help with such a huge and frightening task was an enormous comfort.

Plus, there was just something so *sweet* about a man threatening murder for you. *Big man is good, like him much,* Lena murmured in my head. *No more sad with him.*

"Whoever it was might be dangerous, Orn," I said softly, carding my fingers through his thick chest hair. "They took almost an entire coven, and they—they b-burned our home down."

Orn frowned, a dark inferno behind his eyes. His gaze was pointed towards the far wall, but was clearly focused on something else, something only he could see. His hands gripped me more firmly, pulling me tight against him. He was burning up, feverish, every muscle taut. "They...burned your home down?" He began growling, the sound so low I almost couldn't hear it. His nostrils flared as he met my eyes. "I must *destroy* them, Sara. I *must.*"

I should probably have told him "no", should have grabbed all my things and run off into the storm rather than stay in the company of someone so quick to promise violence. But that wasn't what I did.

"If you have to go, then you're not going alone," I told him, narrowing my eyes when he opened his mouth to protest. "How will you even find your way to our hamlet without me? How will you hunt for clues with no knowledge of the—of the victims?" As soon as the words left my mouth they felt good, a bloody promise of my own twining with his.

"You're still recovering," he protested, but I could feel his resolve to leave me here starting to weaken.

"I'm fine," I insisted, leaning closer. "If I'm going to let you do this, Orn, then I'm a part of it. No matter what, I'm coming with. So your choices are these: try to bind me here, which will not work unless you drug me and leave me incapable of spellwork..." He blanched, and I pressed on: "...or you can bring me with. Let me help, let me..let me have some small vengeance."

He looked into my eyes for long minutes, then sighed, bending awkwardly to rest his forehead against mine. "Alright, Sara. I know it's your fight by rights, that I'm forcing my way somewhere I might not be wanted, but you're letting me lead, and you're letting me carry you. It'll be faster and easier that way, unless you've got power enough to stop the storm *and* melt the several feet of snowfall. Do we have an agreement?"

I frowned at him, not liking the idea of being babied like that in the slightest...but if I was being honest with myself, I wasn't exactly keen on slogging through the snow, either. I nodded, tilting my face closer to kiss him again. It shouldn't feel so good to kiss him, not with those tusks, but somehow it did, and I couldn't stop taking every opportunity to do so. "I must be crazy, but...it's a deal, big guy," I murmured against his mouth, and he grunted, getting to his feet and offering me a hand up.

"Then we'll get ready. You finish eating and I'll assemble a pack."

I managed a small smile, adrenaline beginning to buzz through my body. "Whatever you say, honey," I told him, snagging my plate of nibbled-on food. When I turned back to him he was smiling at me in a way that the world "feral" only just began to capture.

"I like it when you call me that," he growled, every inch of him painted in manic fury. My pussy clenched on nothing, heat creeping up my neck.

"Then I'll have to make sure I do it a lot," I rasped, picking up a bite of apple cake with my fingers and putting it into my mouth as lewdly as I could manage, with far more moaning and licking than was in any way necessary.

I was gratified when his eyes rolled up and he shivered.

Since we were both still naked I was treated to the sight his great green spear of a cock flushed and leaking for me just from that.

"You will be the sweetest death," he said, stomping over to the front door with a dopey grin ghosting at the corners of his lips. He threw it open and then dove into the frigid drifts, making me laugh so hard I nearly choked on my bite of cake.

Within minutes of getting underway, I was blessing all the gods for Orn's stubborn insistence on carrying me. Though the wind and the snow had eased, the cold was sharper and more bitter than ever, and being strapped to Orn's big warm body might have been the only reason I didn't die from exposure. He had been warm before, but the blood song was gradually turning him into a furnace, heat pouring off him in a delicious blanket that eased the biting cold. He had me bound to his front, a huge pack taking up all of the real estate of his back, and at first it felt humiliating to be spread out and pinned to him, but between his soothing warmth and the addictive musk of his scent flavoring my every breath...

Yeah, I was fine with this.

Lena sent me another snaky farewell from the cabin, our mental link too weakened by distance to be more than a feeling and a whiff of an image, but my heart twinged anyway. This cold was no place for my reptilian familiar, but it still felt wrong to leave her behind. Beyond her friendship and her comfort, what if I needed her for spellwork? She was both my conduit and my anchor to the natural world, and without her, I may have lost myself to the aether, or failed to reach it when I needed it most. It made me panic, shivers wracking my body that had nothing to do with the cold. But it was only by Vitrin's grudging mercy that she'd survived that first trip, and the unknowns that I was anxious about confronting without her could make this trip even *more* dangerous to her. Ultimately, losing her was a risk I wasn't willing to take.

Somehow sensing my unease, Orn's big arms wrapped around my body, squeezing me tight against him, and I sank into his comfort, so, so thankful for it I could have cried. One hand rubbed my back while the other yanked his scarf down from his nose and mouth so he could press a kiss between my eyes, which was the only exposed skin on my entire body.

"We'll find the bastards who did this and make them pay, sweetheart," he said over the wind. "I'll not let anything happen to you. I swear it to all the gods, Sara. Not a hair on your head will see harm."

I wriggled until I could press my mittened hands flat to his huge chest, his heart beating a wild, insistent rhythm against my palms even with the layers of fabric between us. "I know," I said, and I was startled by just how much I meant it. Why was it so easy to trust this half-mad orc? But then something else occurred to me, and one of my hands slid up to press to the side of his face. "But you can't come to any harm, either." I narrowed my eyes, trying to sit taller and look firm despite being strapped to him like a little baby. "If you get hurt then I'm vulnerable and —and it'll hurt me, to see you...like that." My cheeks flamed, and I was glad he couldn't see it beneath my own scarf, still snugged over the lower half of my face.

Orn froze mid-stride, his dark eyes boring into mine, stealing my breath and stirring things that had charred to ash when I came upon my destroyed home. *What is this?* I wondered, panic and want warring in my aching chest. Then he seemed to shake off whatever had come over him, his face flushing deeply as he re-situated his scarf on his face.

"I said what I said," he barked, but his eyes were soft when he looked at me. "So just get comfortable, lass, aye?"

I bit my lip under my scarf and nodded, wrapping my limbs around him tight and leaning my cheek against his chest, catching the barest glimpses of the forest past the lengths of fabric that made up my wrap.

It had been difficult for me to remember much about the path my navigation spell had taken me on from my coven's ruined hamlet to Orn's cabin, but Lena had been a surprising help in plotting out a rough map before we'd set off. She'd been tucked under my clothes, blind to the outside world, but her incredible sense of smell had picked up many helpful scents. She'd scented a wolf pack, the only one on this mountain, according to Orn, because he'd made sure he knew their territory well. A copse of honey pine, the metallic bite of fresh-cut ironwood, and moldering apple also proved helpful, and by the end of it Orn was fairly confident he knew the route I'd taken and could retrace it.

The more time I spent with Orn, the more I liked him. He was sweet and kind, but he knew how to bite and growl when the situation called for it. Yes, he was handsome and strapping and had an incredible cock, but when my mind wandered back to our mind-blowing sex, it was his care and intensity that had left the strongest impression. I'd been with other attractive people who were skilled in bed, but I'd never felt that connected to any of them during our couplings. Had never felt so...*worshipped.*

I squirmed a little, my pussy throbbing with interest at the memory of Orn's attentions, and when the friction of my clothes' seam felt delicious against my clit I found myself doing it again before I could help myself. *Now is* not *the time, Sara,* I chided myself, forcing my hips to still.

"Are you uncomfortable? Do you need to stop?" Orn asked, and I flushed, knowing we'd barely been walking for an hour and here I was derailing things with my wandering mind and poor impulse control.

"No, I'm fine," I squeaked out, cursing how not-fine I sounded. Sure enough, Orn stopped walking, hefting me a little higher so he could look in my eyes.

"Are you certain you're well, sweetheart? We can stop whenever you want. We're already doing well with time." One huge hand came up to palm the back of my head through our layers of protection, and for some reason his tenderness only made me feel more needy. *What is it about this orc?!*

I squirmed again, the satisfaction of my clit rubbing against my clothes far too short-lived. Orn dropped his scarf again, presumably to see me better, but as soon as his lower face was revealed his nostrils flared, dark eyes going darker as his pupils blew wide.

"Ah, I see now," he growled, plunging forward until my back pressed into a tree. "My sweet little witch is in *need.*"

CHAPTER ELEVEN

Claimed

ORN

When the blood song had first begun its strumming, I'd thought that perhaps the powerful lust for Sara that had taken me over utterly would fade to the background.

I was wrong.

My need for her was only *whetted* by my newfound drive for vengeance, it would seem, every nerve attuned to her warmth, her scent, the plush press of her body against mine. But I felt less like a beast knowing that she was just as affected, her hot cunt against my belly needing to be filled as much as my hard cock wanted to fill her. She panted my name as I pressed her to the nearest tree, and a surge of desire barreled through me so strongly that I feared for a moment that my legs would give out.

Distantly, I wondered at our sudden attraction, at why it should be that she made me lose myself so thoroughly, but the bulk of my consciousness knew it didn't matter; she wanted me as much as I wanted her, and that meant that I was free to taste her over and over again, as many times as she'd let me, even if it meant losing myself in the process. Besides—what would I *really* be losing in such a bargain? Loneliness and a lack of belonging? Crippling shyness when it came to humans, especially women? Solitude so deep it drove me mad more often than not?

Being Sara's thrall was far better.

Sara wriggled against me, grinding her cunt into the seam of her borrowed leggings, faint whimpers carrying to me through her scarf and over the howl of the wind. The very *cold* wind, and I frowned when I realized I would not be able to strip her bare and taste every inch of her. I bit down on my right mitten and used my mouth to tear it off, immediately shoving it under the wraps that held her against me, then between our bodies, burrowing carefully through her clothes until I felt soft skin against mine. I let my hand finish warming up against her belly before tunneling lower, carding through her damp curls until I found my slick, swollen prize.

At the first careful graze of my finger on her clit she cried out and bucked into my touch, her head sinking back to rest against the tree trunk. "Orn," she said, her eyes dazed on mine, and I used my other hand to tug her scarf low enough to claim her mouth in a kiss, needing her scent and her flavor all over my skin, needing to couple my breaths with hers, to twine as much of myself with her as the weather allowed. I wanted to swallow her pleasure, my mouth intense and eager on hers, but she matched my movements and my intensity easily, her hands coming up to cup my face and hold me in place.

Her hips began to roll and buck, guiding my fingers exactly where she needed them, her thick thighs squeezing my sides like a rider directing their mount, and I groaned low in my throat, overwhelmed by her beauty, her power, with the very fact that she was in my arms and finding her pleasure from me.

Mine.

The thought reverberated around and around inside my skull, building in strength just as Sara's pleasure built. Her rhythm faltered, no longer able to kiss me as she panted and moaned instead, and I rested my forehead against hers as I continued to work her. I appeared to be saying things, though I had no conscious recollection of deciding to do so: "That's it, sweetheart. Use me. I'm all yours, you take everything you want. I'll give you everything you need, Sara. You're so beautiful, I can't stand it. I need you to come for me. *Please.*" On and on I babbled, but Sara must have liked it, because she reached her peak with a keen, her clit throbbing against my fingers, wetness seeping up and all over my skin. I shuddered with her, the rock-hard bar in my pants twitching and oozing helplessly. I wanted nothing more than to plunge into her, but it would hold us up too long to set up a camp.

Sara blinked up at me, dazed, then smiled and surged up until she could kiss me again, her round cheeks pressing against my tusks in a way that shouldn't feel special or good but *did*, in the mysterious way that so many things seemed to when it came to this little witch. This kiss was different from the rabid consumption of before; this was sweetness and soft heat, gentleness and care, free from desperation. It felt so good, but it ripped something open in my chest that ached and stole my breath, the sudden urge to weep flitting through me. Luckily, it didn't last, my mind instead focusing on Sara.

"Hold me up, honey," she murmured against me when her lips left mine. I gripped her under her thighs automatically, hoisting her higher.

"Are you uncomfortable?" I asked, wanting her to be well and comfortable but more than a little distracted by the blood song and my intense arousal.

She nodded, her arms disappearing into the wraps and fumbling around where I couldn't see them. "Yeah, I'm fine. I just want to...see something."

My brow furrowed, trying to catch a glimpse of what she was doing, but it was too dark under the wraps to catch sight of much.

"See what? Can I help?"

She grinned at me devilishly, and then I felt her hands at the laces of my pants, untying them and tugging them loose with a dexterity that shocked me. She tugged me loose moments later, giving me a stroke and biting her lip as she looked up into my face.

My eyes rolled up into my head, pleasure piercing me like a bolt. I sagged forward with a groan, my hips twitching, trying to fuck into her tiny little hand.

I was so lost in sensation that it took several moments for the fact that she was saying my name to register. *"Orn!"* she said again, her hand stilling and squeezing my length to get my attention. I opened my eyes and felt myself flush hot.

"I'm sorry," I managed to grit out, my hips still twitching helplessly.

"Lower me down again," she told me, her impish grin still in place. "I have a surprise for you."

I did as she asked, wondering what her surprise could possibly be, when all at once my cockhead met searing, sopping-wet softness that parted for me easily, almost eagerly, and in a flash I understood.

"H-how?" I asked, my knees going too weak to hold us up anymore, so that I was kneeling in the snow, Sara's cunt gripping me tight and fluttering at my intrusion. "How...*pants?*"

Somehow, she understood what I meant, rocking her hips to drive me deeper. "I got them out of the way," she said huskily, doing her best to get the leverage to work herself on me. "Don't worry about that. Worry about the fact that I need you to *move*, Orn."

Her words unleashed me, and I sat up higher on my knees, wedging Sara against the tree once more, pinning her there so that I could rut up into her senselessly. My mind was blank except for that litany of *mine* that only grew louder and more insistent the harder I pounded into her, with every pleasure-soaked cry that flew from her lips. She felt so good, so *right*, and despite already having more orgasms in a single day than I'd ever had before, I felt yet another barreling down on me, rippling down my spine and along every nerve with furious, brutal intensity. Sara was so dripping wet that I needed hardly any force to wedge my knot into her, slipping past her entrance to lodge inside her with a small pop, my sac wrenching up hard and my cock emptying into her. My breath caught at the intensity, but then I was roaring, my throat roughed up and raw from the sound, and after a few seconds I realized I was saying something, that I was shouting my claim on Sara into the wilds.

"Mine!"

No sooner did I realize what I was saying than Sara was reaching her own peak, her scream joining mine, weaving through it and making a beautiful sort of song, her sweet cunt clamping onto me, milking my shaft and squeezing every drop from my knot.

Our orgasms seemed to go on for minutes, hours, maybe even days, my hands gripping her body and my mouth on hers the only thing that felt real in all the world. It took a long time to come back to my senses, and when I did I realized that I was still panting "mine" at her in between desperate, feverish kisses.

And Sara, my beautiful little witch, so perfect in every way, was saying something, too:

"Yours," she sighed, "All yours, Orn. My sweet honey."

CHAPTER TWELVE

Accepted

SARA

Should I have been worried about what had just happened? Not the mind-blowing, earth-shattering orgasm, obviously. But unless my brains were more scrambled than I'd thought, there'd been a whole lot of shouting at the end there about Orn thinking he owned me.

But I wasn't scared, or angry, or any sane sort of emotion like that. No, my crazy mess was *into it*. The thought of belonging to this man turned me on and made me feel warm and tingly all over. I guess that was why I'd gone along with it, had agreed with him and told him I was his.

But could I even promise that? I wasn't out here for fun—I was looking for my stolen coven, my only family in the world after my parents had died to fever when I was still a baby. It felt like I was spitting all over everything Mother Tonn had done to care for me. And Brekka, my best friend—what would she think of me making such huge promises to someone I'd just met?

But then I opened my eyes, my vision filled with a handsome, broad green face. Inky lashes rested on flushed cheeks, tusked mouth hanging open and swallowing up huge breaths that I felt echoed in the chest pressed tight to mine. I could feel his heartbeat, too, even through layers of clothes. And there was a little crease that had formed between his thick black brows, something about it so sweet it made me ache. His full lips trembled a little as he fought to catch his breath, and once again, I melted into him.

"You okay, honey?" I leaned in to press my forehead to his, letting our fogging breaths mingle in the frigid air. His cock, still buried impossibly deep inside me—where I now knew it would stay until his knot deflated—bucked at the sound of my voice. He really liked when I talked sweet to him.

"I...yes. Gods, I think you broke me, but in the best way." He grinned, lines forking out from the corners of his eyes. I wanted to kiss those lines, and the one between his brows, and every other inch of warm green skin my lips could reach. But I'd done enough to hold up our rescue mission.

"I'm sorry," I chuckled, finally feeling Orn slip free and wincing at the rush of hot fluid. " I seem to have made a mess of you," I grinned. With how we were positioned, most of our cum wound up in his lap.

"Sweetheart, you can make as much of a mess out of me as you want..." Coal-dark eyes raised to look deep into mine, the intensity of emotion there stealing my breath. "You can have me any way you want, for as long as you want. I'm all yours, Sara."

A lump formed in my throat that took several swallows to dislodge. I used the excuse of fixing our pants and helping him clean up to mask my sudden silence.

"I...I'm very flattered, Orn." Gods, this was a bad conversation to be having strapped together with his cum still running out of my pussy. "But...we barely know each other. You don't know that I'm deserving of that kind of...devotion." *And I have no idea if you're a dangerous madman hiding from the law in these mountains.* Suddenly, I felt very foolish, and more than a little scared. What had I done?

Orn got to his feet with a soft grunt, shrugging before setting himself back to rights. "I know all I need to," he said, readjusting me and our pack. "I know I've never felt like this before about anyone. I know you've awakened the blood song in me when twenty years of Orcish tactics did nothing. And if it's all a spell you've cast on me, I *still* don't care. This is the happiest I think I've ever been." His voice was light and easy, if a little muffled by his scarf and the wind.

"Of course, I don't expect you to trust me just like that." He tried to snap his fingers, forgetting about his thick mittens. "Er, anyway—that's why I'm leaving it up to you. So we can be to each other whatever feels most comfortable to you."

I bit my lip behind my own scarf. "What if I want to leave when this is all done?"

His dark eyes were sad, but one side crinkled in a smile all the same. "Then that's it. I'll miss you something fierce, I suspect. But if that's your choice, then that's your choice."

I felt nothing but truth in his words, my muscles finally releasing the tension his sudden confession had brought on. I smiled at him, hoping my eyes showed it. "I...I think I'd miss you too," I admitted, shocked by how much I meant it. I cupped the side of his face with one of my own mittens. "And don't worry, I haven't cast a spell on you. I'd never do something like that."

"If you say so, little witch," he winked, his gait easing into a regular rhythm now that we were on our way. I shot him a glare, but he didn't seem to notice it, and it wasn't long before the warmth of his body and the motion of his walking lulled me to sleep.

I awoke an unclear amount of time later to Orn's gentle prodding.

"Hello, my pretty one," he said softly, and despite the strangeness of our situation I found myself smiling wide, a fluttering lightness in my chest. "Are you hungry? Thirsty?"

I smacked my lips, realizing I was, in fact, very much both of those things. I nodded, my stomach giving a very timely rumble, and Orn untied us and set me down with a chuckle.

Even though I hadn't been doing any of the work in retracing my journey to find my stolen coven, my body protested with quite a lot of cracking and popping as I clambered down, the muscles in my thighs shivery and sore. But the complaints of my mortal tether were soon forgotten in the frenzy that was Orn feeding me.

The man seemed to think I was still as exhausted and starving as I'd been when I first stumbled through his door, with how he shoved morsel after morsel at me. It didn't seem like that much food should have fit into our pack, but more kept coming: cheeses and two kinds of hard bread, nuts, dried fruit, jerky, bars of something Orcish Orn called *setha*, and more that I insisted I was too full to even look at. Orn was a big person and should have easily outpaced me, but it took my threatening violence to get him to eat more than a few nibbles. It was like he was worried we'd run out, and he wanted me to have it all. The fact that he'd packed enough for a week when we wouldn't be traveling for longer than two days didn't seem to factor into those feelings.

Once Orn was finally eating, I got up and looked around, taking in the forest beyond the shallow cave Orn had found for us to rest in. It wasn't warm, being little more than a dip in the ice-crusted black rock of the cliff wall, but it was out of the wind and got less snow than the open ground beyond. Once I was more awake, I could throw together a sheltering spell that would make it more comfortable.

I peered through the white haze of the storm, trying in vain to pick out something familiar, to see at least some small part of the trail Orn was following, but it was useless; all the trees I could see looked no different from any other in the forests carpeting the feet of the Kellaides Mountains.

"Do you think they're still alive?' I found myself asking softly, my arms folding tight across my chest. Orn looked up from his jerky, broad jaw working hard to break down his mouthful of the leathery meat. He seemed to actually consider it, and when he swallowed and got to his feet I appreciated that he didn't look at me with pity.

"I think that even in the worst-case scenario, more will be alive than dead. But to my thinking, they're probably all still alive. Otherwise, why go to the trouble of taking them alive in the first place? If they wanted them dead—" Orn cut himself off with a cough, his eyes leaving mine for a brief moment.

If they just wanted them dead—us dead, really, since they probably had no idea they'd missed me—they would have massacred the coven then and there. It was awful, but the most horrible thing about it was that it was the truth.

"I'm sorry, sweetheart," he murmured, taking a half step forward and reaching for me. I buried my face in his broad chest, squeezing back tears and soaking in the sweetness of his comfort. I loved the smell of him, the solidness, the warmth. There was something about him that soothed me on an almost primal level. His large hands rubbed my back while he continued to murmur soft, sweet things, and soon I was no longer in danger of breaking down into tears that I feared would never end once they started.

I kissed him softly and pulled away, digging into my pack for the reagents I'd need for the sheltering spell. It was a simple spell, but very handy: it would block out most of the bitter wind without trapping our fire's smoke, and would shield said fire from being seen outside our little campsite. It felt like nothing in the face of all that Orn had done for me, but the big guy was absolutely beside himself with amazement.

"And you can just *do* things like that? Like it's nothing?" he asked for the third time, stepping from one side of the boundary line I'd drawn to the other to take in the full effect of the spell. "Sweet Delenaa, that's *amazing*, Sara!"

"Well, not just *any* time. I need the right ingredients and enough energy to cast it."

He nodded, considering. "You know, I've never asked it, but what *is* it about witches that scares people so, when mages are treated so fairly?" He settled behind me, long legs bracketing mine and strong arms pulling me into his big body. I snuggled into him, my gaze on the banked fire. "Perhaps this is just a part of your enthrallment spell, but you seem very kind and tame to me," he said, his deep voice light and teasing.

I snorted. "What do you mean, 'enthrallment spell'?"

I felt him shrug. "Well, I figured out that you must have felt the need to warn me of your witching ways because you planned to take me as your thrall. And given my ever-growing passion, it feels obvious that you succeeded. But you needn't fear, my sweet; I am far happier than I have ever been under your spell."

I couldn't decide if the proper response was amusement or outrage, so I settled on laughing while twisting in his arms and swatting at whatever I could reach. He brayed with laughter, holding me tightly but allowing me to smack his arms and shoulders in indignation. "I would *never—*" SMACK "*ever—*" SMACK "do that kind of spellwork on a person!" SMACK-SMACK-SMACK.

"Aye, I know, lass!" he gasped, wiping tears of mirth from where they clung to his thick dark lashes. "But you have to admit the timing is suspicious…"

After we'd settled down, Orn thoroughly chastised and just as thoroughly kissed, I sighed deeply, letting myself settle back into the cradle of his body and steep in the warmth and comfort of him. "It's silly superstition and old biases," I began, returning to his question from earlier. "Mages can channel aether—that's magical energy, if you didn't know—directly. It's an ability you're either born with or not. Witches are connected to aether, can sense it and use it, but not directly. We need to harness the aether found in nature, to extract it and coax it into doing what we want."

Orn hummed thoughtfully. "That doesn't sound so bad," he rumbled, kissing me just under my ear. "What's so frightening about that?"

"Well, it's not *just* that," I hedged, biting my lip. Orn's kisses were starting to distract me, to heat up my body yet again. "Long ago, there was a sect of witches who turned to a side of magic that most of us refuse to touch. Dark magic...blood magic." Orn's lips stilled, but he didn't move away. I chose to take that as a good sign. "It was a very few number of us, and it was generations ago at this point, but the fear remains. It probably doesn't help that all witches are women, and that the rise of the One God has meant that that fact condemns us almost as much as the witchery does.

"No modern witch has any interest in the dark side of magic, but the damage is done. And now—" My throat began to burn, feeling so tight I worried I wouldn't be able to talk anymore. "My coven is my *family*, Orn," I managed in a ragged whisper. "I never knew my birth family. If—if they're gone—"

"Then I will go and fetch them from the beyond." His large arms tightened around me, squeezing me close. "But even if the worst comes to pass, I swear to you, on all the gods, on my honor, on life itself: you will never again be alone. If nothing else, you'll have me. I just hope that that's acceptable to you."

"You idiot," I sobbed, turning in his arms to throw my arms around his neck and bury my face into his warm green skin. "It's better than 'acceptable'. It's—it's *everything*." I pulled away just enough to meet his obsidian eyes. "Thank you, Orn. I... gods, I truly will never be able to repay you for everything you've done. You're so...so *good*."

He tucked a loose curl behind my ear, smiling softly. "Now who's being foolish? You are worth any price I might have to pay. I've been waiting for you my whole life, Sara. I just didn't know it until you showed up on my doorstep."

This time when we kissed, it was like swallowing fire and honey. His warmth, his scent, the sounds he made oh-so-softly when I touched him, wrapped around me and drenched me in their sweetness. His lips and tongue swept away my hesitations, my doubts, until there was only one bright, crystalline thing: Orn was mine, and I was his.

It wasn't long after that that I found myself in his lap again, writhing and grinding into his big body like I was trying to start a fire with my pussy. Orn groaned low in his throat, his chest rumbling against my sensitive, aching breasts, heavy with arousal. There was far too much fabric between us. I peeled off my layers in one clumsy go, baring myself to him. His hands came up to cup and knead my breasts, his callouses adding a delicious friction that had me aching and drenched. I reached between us, going for the ties of Orn's leather pants, but his hand caught my wrist before I could reach them.

"I think if I come one more time today my cock'll fall off, sweetheart," he chuckled, redirecting my hand to his tunic laces. "But I have other ways of taking care of my mate." He started, realizing what he'd said, his eyes widening as he made a choking sound.

I felt breathless, stunned by that one little word. *Mate*. It wasn't a term to be throw around lightly, and for Orn to use it to refer to me...

Well, it certainly explained some things. As if it were illustrating the situation, I felt my wet hot need dribble out of my throbbing pussy to trail down my inner thigh. I took one breath, then two. And when I looked into his dark eyes all I felt was calm.

Alright, then. Guess I was an orc's mate. "Yes," I breathed, unable to pull any other word forward. "*Yes*, Orn."

His panic ebbed, the wild need from before rekindling. "Yes?" he asked, his hands on my body stroking and caressing me once more.

I nodded, pressing myself closer to him. "Yes."

I tore at his shirt laces, baring his broad, hairy chest and soft stomach. My mouth watered at the sight of him, at the contrast between power and gentleness that colored everything about this surprising man. In the flickering firelight, I could *just* make it out when he blushed at my scrutiny. He reached for the ties of my own pants, undoing them quickly. He told me to stand, and I obeyed, letting him pull the thick pants down and off my legs. I shivered, chill air pebbling my skin and peaking my nipples even while the fire warmed my back. Orn frowned at my shiver, pulling me closer and rubbing warmth into my skin with his hands.

Without a word, he guided me to the bedroll and coaxed me onto my back, covering my naked body with the thick wool blanket—silky-soft because it was aerlanis wool—before slipping under it himself and slithering down my body. I shivered again, but this time in heady anticipation.

Once Orn's face was aligned with my mound, most of his lower half was exposed to the elements, but since he'd left his pants and boots on he likely didn't feel it. Tender kisses and nuzzles began to pepper my skin, his hot mouth worshipful as he tasted my thighs, my heavy lower belly, my mons. I found myself lifting my hips up into his gentle caresses, wanting more. But Orn would not give it, his touch staying soft and sweet and oh-so-maddening.

I whined, my hands slipping into his thick hair and trying to guide him to where I wanted him, where I *needed* him. Despite everything we'd already done together, I was still once again desperate for him.

I heard a throaty chuckle beneath the crackle and pop of the low-burning flames, big hands sliding under my ass to lift me and knead my flesh. I said nothing, his hot breath fanning over the sensitive skin of my pussy, the moisture that had pooled there turning the heat cool. Slowly, too slowly, *maddeningly slowly*, his mouth drifted to my throbbing clit, no amount of pulling or shoving from me making any sort of difference in his pace.

I should just tell him to hurry up and get to it, I thought, frustrated instead of satisfied now that his mouth was finally on me—because he was still going so slowly, so gently, when I wanted *more.* But for some reason, I didn't say anything—I let him tease me, let him keep me on the brink of insanity. I was curious about what he was planning, for one, but there was also an element of trust there. I may not have known who his parents were, or the name of wherever he'd been born, or even how old he was (gods, I hoped he was as adult as he looked), but I knew this was a good person who cared about me and seemed as concerned with making me feel good as some other people cared about breathing. He wouldn't leave me aching and wanting.

And sure enough, he did not; one moment he was all light touches and softness, and the next two thick fingers were dipping into my entrance, carefully coating themselves in my essence, before plunging deep inside me. Like iron to a lodestone, they found that sweet something deep inside of me that made me feel like I was floating, rocking and stroking up into it.

I squeaked, going rigid for just a moment at the suddenness of Orn's delicious invasion, before letting out a gasp and a moan as he finally, *finally,* began working me up properly.

His mouth on my clit grew firmer, the flat of his tongue moving in quick circles over the hood of that sensitive bud. I was already so wound up from his teasing that the few licks that had wound up on the exposed underside of my clit had been too much, and somehow the mad orc *knew that.*

And I'm *supposed to be the witch,* I managed to think between the bursts of starlight lighting me up under Orn's focused attention. I choked back a laugh, realizing that this man was literally fucking me stupid. *Too much blood getting diverted from my brain,* and at that thought I *did* giggle. I expected him to stop, to ask me what was so funny, but he didn't. He just cocked a thick black brow at me when I lifted the blanket to take a peek at him and redoubled his efforts.

Any laughter choked off entirely, my body coiling tight as steel and aching to release. I panted and moaned, swearing as I clutched helplessly as his thick hair. My eyes fluttered closed, my back arching and my hips undulating up into his mouth. I was helpless to stop it, my body no longer entirely under my control, as Orn wrapped his lips tight around my clit and sucked.

I came with a cry so loud I heard it echo, the bliss of my orgasm so sharp and sweet my mind shattered. I went to another plane of existence, everything small and insignificant in the face of the waves of pleasure barreling through me. And Orn, that great and terrible fiend, was still working me, his movements gentle once more, but firm and insistent, and sure enough—

"Orn, fuck, oh gods, please, no, please, ohfuckohgodsoh—"

And I was screaming once more, my throat raw, as the tight coil of my muscles released all at once. I'd still been throbbing and weak from the first orgasm, but that orc, my sweet Orn, had worked some magic on my body that had my body rallying and coming hot and hard. Heat and glitter thrummed through me, warm wetness gushing from my core, and for one mad moment I thought it might be my spirit leaving my mortal flesh.

If anyone was going to be able to fuck me to death, it would be Orn. I knew that with the certainty that I knew the sun would rise in the morning.

He was still parked between my thighs, growling and moaning as he lapped up every drop of my slick that he could find, his blade of a nose nuzzling my flesh and his fingers still buried deep inside me, stroking my sweet spot.

"Orn," I said weakly, my voice a raw rasp that even I could barely hear. "Orn," I said louder, throwing the blanket off of us both. He ignored me, or perhaps was beyond hearing me, and I whimpered as I felt another orgasm begin to flick at the ends of my nerves, a hungry fire that I was certain would burn me to ash if I let him kindle it. I shoved at his head, using every ounce of strength left in my wrung-out muscles and *still* only just managing to push hard enough to get his attention; moving him was impossible. "*Orn!*"

He growled again, his dark eyes and hair wild. I swallowed, half from nerves, half to try and restore my voice. "Down, boy," I told him, sitting up on an elbow so I could reach him better. I grabbed a fistful of his hair and held it tight. "I need a break, honey. Can you calm down?"

I thought I heard another growl—bloody gods, this blood song was something else—but he nodded, pressing his face into my wrist and kissing it softly. "I'm sorry, Sara."

I flopped onto my back, laughing weakly. "It's alright, sweetness. It was amazing. Just…too much."

"When can I taste you again?" he asked, his voice a low rumble that shivered along my exposed thighs.

Again? "You want to do it again? Honey, I'm flattered, but I don't know if I have any more in me tonight. And shouldn't we be resting up, getting ready for tomorrow?" By Orn's estimation, we were close—he'd begun to catch the scent of our hamlet, my fading scent mingling with sharp herbs and sweet woodsmoke, with the bright tang of magic and the sour rank of fear. Or so he said; I could smell none of it. And while we'd eaten and cleaned up a bit, there was still gear to check over and potentially repair, reagents I needed to work on for ready-made spellwork once we found my coven, and sweet Delenaa, *we just plain needed rest!*

Orn frowned, shooting my pussy a longing look that was almost comical, before he got to his feet and stepped beyond the light of the fire. He ignored my confused calls, passing through the barrier I'd made and into the howling storm. Naked from the waist up, he lifted his arms from his sides and tilted his head back, before tipping backwards and falling into a thick drift of snow with a gentle crunch and a *whump*. He lay there for several minutes, making me worry something was wrong, but just as I was pulling on my clothes to go to him, he rose, shivering and damp but looking much calmer.

"Sorry, sweetheart," he said, rubbing the back of his neck and looking sheepish. "I got uh…carried away."

"Are you alright?"

He nodded, flushing, and then settled by the fire once more. He pulled a blanket around his shoulders and left his legs spread wide and bent at the knees. "Will you sit with me?" he asked, holding out one huge hand.

I smiled, all but falling to the ground and settling between his legs once more. He adjusted the blanket to cover me, too, then sighed and melted against me.

"When we find your people, what will you do next?"

"You mean me?"

"No, I mean all of you. The whole coven." He paused. "How many of you are there?"

"Every coven has twelve. It is a sacred number, and precious enough to the gods that no matter what, a coven stays at twelve from its creation to its dissolution. Which hopefully never comes, but it *has* happened, from what the Mothers have said."

Orn hummed thoughtfully, pressing a kiss to the side of my head. "You have more than one mother?"

I shook my head. "Not in the literal sense. It's what we call our elders, our leaders. Usually there are three, though they are not always the oldest among us. Gretta, for example, is older than Mother Tonn by at least a decade, but she's not a Mother herself."

"Fascinating, I had no idea. And this is just how it works out?"

I smiled, easing back into his warmth as my eyes slipped closed. He had many questions for me, some I had no answers for, like how it was that we knew about the sacred numbers, or who had first discovered the spell structures and what reagents they needed to work. His curiosity sparked my own, and I realized that there was much about my life as a witch that I had taken for granted, that I had made commonplace and never bothered to wonder about. I vowed I would find those answers, for myself as much as him, as I told him all I could.

I didn't remember falling asleep, but woke to Orn's gentle snoring and the shrill calls of frost doves welcoming the dawn.

CHAPTER THIRTEEN

Something Stinks

ORN

We made good time, stumbling into the clearing that swaddled Sara's hamlet before the sun had gotten fully above the tree line. It was a small and simple place, but sweet and welcoming for all its roughness. The scents that I'd been following were stronger here, but fast-fading, and I knew that we needed to hurry after the trail, or risk losing it. I had hoped to give Sara time here to rest and gather herself, but it was looking like that would have to wait.

The smoke was long gone, and most of the charred remains of buildings were buried under mounds of snow, but the scent of woodsmoke and fire was still heavy enough on the air that no doubt Sara could smell it too. But that wasn't why I was in such a rush to leave—what worried me was that there was too much rust and iron on the air. And something else, something sour and acrid like bile, but less...organic. My instinct was to hide it from Sara, to protect her, but I was thinking clearly enough to know that that was foolish. Why should I hide information from my mate? Especially one as strong and capable as Sara?

"Orn, can you come here?" she called from the western edge

of the ruined hamlet.

She was squatting beside a lump in the snow, a heavy frown marring her beautiful face. I lowered myself beside her, going still when I realized that the strange odor was much stronger here. And the snow was too thin; the rest of the area was heavily blanketed, but this patch was covered in barely more than a dusting. Sara used a rag to brush away more snow from the lump, revealing a dead rabbit.

It had not been a clean kill, the suffering of the creature plain even in death. Bits and pieces of the poor thing were scattered around it, gradually revealed by Sara's careful brushing with the rag, and after a moment I realized there was a pattern to the way the offal was scattered. I swallowed bile.

This had been intentional.

"Vitrin's mercy, what *is* this?" I asked, an irrepressible growl rumbling under my words.

I hadn't expected an answer, but Sara gave one anyway. "Looks a bit like blood magic, but more...gods, it's like it's *unnatural*, somehow. There's this—this *taste* to it that makes me sick."

Lead settled in my gut, the hairs on the back of my neck rising. "There's a strange scent here, too. I've never encountered it before, but it is somewhat like how you're describing. It should be natural, but it's not."

Sara pinched the bridge of her nose, squeezing her eyes shut. "Bloody gods, what *happened* here?"

I placed a hand on her shoulder and squeezed. "Whatever it was, we are on our way to undo it. The scent of blood is weak, scattered. This is the strongest the scent is in the whole of the hamlet."

Sara leaned into my touch, covering my hand with one of hers. "So they were hopefully alive when they were taken from here," she croaked. Her big brown eyes slid closed, several deep breaths fogging in the chill air. When she opened her eyes again they were glazed with tears, but burning with fury, with determination.

I could not possibly have loved her any more than I did in that moment, seeing her beauty tempered in fire and wrath. My cock stirred in my pants, but the abuse I'd delivered yesterday made the feeling too aching to want to do anything about it except make it go away.

I stood, holding my hand out for my mate. She took it, and came easily to her feet. "Is there enough of a trail for you to follow?" she asked.

I nodded, scenting the laden air carefully. "Aye. But it's fading fast, love. We'll need to move quickly. Are you tired?"

"No." She bit her lip, huffing in frustration. "A little," she admitted, clearly unhappy about it. "Mostly my legs are stiff and sore."

I clucked my tongue sadly. "I'm sorry, sweetheart."

One brow arched, a saucy smile curving her lips out of their frown. "You should be; it's all *your* fault."

I laughed, grabbing her chin and bending to kiss her. Sweetness burst on my tongue, her scent wrapping around me from our closeness. She melted into me, her arms looping around my neck and pulling us still closer together.

Perhaps my cock was not so reluctant to perform, after all.

"Strap me in, big guy," she murmured against my lips, her pink tongue darting out to lick up one of my tusks. Despite the fact that it had no nerves, I shivered. "We've got to move fast, remember?"

I grunted, too much blood pooled in my groin to string together a sentence. I let go of her long enough to retrieve the wraps that held her to my body, hefting her into place and tying her down quickly. I hauled our pack onto my back, and then we were off, the rank scent of whatever had come here my guide.

"If you stay with me…" I said at length, ducking my head to take a deep breath of her scent, my nose planted in the bend of her neck for long moments. The foul smell I was following was turning my stomach and giving me a headache, and Sara was the sweetest reprieve from it.

"Yes?" she asked, a little breathless. I grinned, nipping her delicate skin gently.

"You'll have to get to used to being carried like this," I continued, straightening with an appreciative smack to her round ass. "I like it too well to give it up."

She laughed, looking up at me with a soft affection that took my breath away.

"I guess I'll just have to learn to live with it, then."

I could have flown, in that moment. There was no way Sara would ever be rid of me, not anymore. If her affections changed, I would respect them...but I would not be able to leave her, even if it meant I followed her from the shadows like a lapdog. She was everything.

She was my mate.

<u>SARA</u>

The sun was swollen with color and nearing the horizon by the time we finally found the bastards who'd taken my coven. There was only one tent with two figures standing near a nearby cave's entrance, both people so heaped with furs it was impossible to tell much about them.

"Only two?" I whispered, my eyes darting to Orn's sharp profile. His jaw was tense, knotted muscles jumping under his deep olive skin. His nostrils flared, taking in the breeze that stirred the thick black strands of hair that had escaped his braid.

He was so beautiful.

After a moment he shook his head, turning his dark eyes to me. "No, the bulk of their force is in the cave. They're... celebrating, I think."

Panic threatened to grind me down, but I took a deep breath, then another, and beat it back once more. But when Orn took my mittened hand and held it tight, I took his comfort gladly. "Can you tell anything about what they're celebrating?"

He shook his head, tusks glinting as they caught the dying light. "No. But the smell of blood is old, and doesn't strike me as human." He sniffed again, closing his eyes to concentrate. Disgust wrinkled his nose, but he seemed to have figured something out. "Deer, I think. Maybe a little rabbit," he told me. My panic subsided further.

"How can you smell all that?" I asked, letting him lead me farther from the encampment. "Is that an orc thing?"

He shrugged. "In a way. My nose is keen, but it's never been this sharp before. Likely it's the blood song." He lead me through the forest until we couldn't see the encampment anymore, parting the heavy snow-laden boughs of a huge pine tree, the branches providing a rough shelter from the wind. "We'll camp here tonight, I think. I'm going to scout some more, try and get a better idea of how many there are."

I snatched his arm and gripped it tight, stopping him as he tried to pull out a tarp for our bedrolls.

"You're going back? Alone? At night?"

Orn's face softened, his free hand cupping my cheek. "My sweet little witch. The gods themselves couldn't tear me away from you."

I swallowed a painful lump. "But they managed to capture most of a coven of talented witches. They're not going to be pushovers, honey."

"Ah, but they had time to prepare for that, to craft that hideous spell they used to smooth their way." He grinned wide, eyes going unfocused as he pictured it. "And they will have never come afoul of an Orcish man with the blood song in his veins and a sweet goddess to worship when the job is done." His gaze returned to me, something wild and dangerous glimmering in his coal-dark eyes. "They won't know what's upon them until it is *far* too late."

I shivered, but not from the cold—this was my first time seeing this side of Orn, and while it should have terrified me, should have sent me running, instead it...it *excited* me. There was so much menace and deadly power in that huge, solid body —but every second with him had shown me that it was all *for* me, for him to use to take care of me, to protect me.

I pressed close and kissed him hard, my arms circling his neck and squeezing tight. "Be careful, you madman," I told him, my voice hoarse from unshed tears. "If I have to go in there by myself and rescue you along with everyone else I will be *so angry.*"

He laughed, kissing me back. Then we parted and got our little camp set up, the night quickly falling to cloak the forest in dark.

CHAPTER FOURTEEN

The Unmaker

ORN

I wasn't lying when I said that Sara had nothing to fear...but it was not the *whole* truth, either. I was nervous about my solo adventure deeper into the strange humans' encampment, and it all had to do with that scent. That unnatural, unholy reek that bathed the entire area and set my teeth on edge. A band of humans, even a lot of humans, was no match for a determined orc in the thrall of the song—and though these might not be normal humans, there was no other option than to scout out the encampment and discover all that I could.

I would just have to be careful. Quiet, small, careful. There was no way I was going to let Sara anywhere near that cave without having a better idea of what we were up against.

But from the beginning, it was obvious that the gods were on my side. The guards posted outside were careless, distracted, and I was able to slip past them so easily I found myself embarrassed on their behalf. Once I was in the cave I was alone, the sounds of merriment coming from much deeper inside; this was a large cave system, then, with several passageways and caverns.

Without the crisp wind and the cut of pine sap to dull the unnatural scent it was almost overwhelming, my stomach turning and threatening to dispose of my supper any time I tried to breathe through my nose. *In Salerah's name, I will cleanse this place of this filth,* I thought, grimacing at a hellish altar I passed. Whatever they were doing here, it was an affront to the very fabric of the world, a stain that was so awful there was no choice but to cut it out entirely.

Howling sounded from around a corner and I froze, pressing myself into the shadowy stone walls. My ears strained, trying to pick out every sound I was hearing and give it a name. The howling was human, I noted, and seemed to be part of the celebration, other voices gradually joining it and weaving through it until it was like a song—a cursed, unreal song that stood my hair on end.

When the noise subsided I was rewarded for my vigilance at last.

"Fucking can't wait for tomorrow," a rough voice said. "Been looking at those cunts for too damn long without being able to do nothing to 'em. But the Unmaker needs fresh, intact meat for 'is journey, aye?"

"That's what Bell said," another voice slurred. Their next words were drowned out by something heavy and metallic crashing to the floor, but I was able to just make out the tail end of it: "…still be warm enough, after."

My pulse drummed heavily through my veins, rage filling me so quickly and furiously that it made me lightheaded. I shuffled back, away from this cavern, before the blood song took all my sense and demanded I slaughter them all here and now, with nothing but my small hunting knife to help be get through all that work. *Foul wretches.*

I checked down two more passageways that forked off from that one, stopping when I heard voices to try and glean what I could. But much of it was the same: their god, this "Unmaker", needed a huge sacrifice to traverse the planes and make its way here, and Sara's coven were meant to be that sacrifice. They were waiting until tomorrow night, when the moon would be new, but the celebrations were already well underway. The only other valuable information was that they slept during the day. That guard *might* be more vigilant, knowing that their brethren were all asleep, but it didn't seem like there would be any more than two.

In all, I thought there might be something like two or three dozen of these animals—I refused to think of such cruel, filthy beasts as people. Certainly, there would be fighters among them, but after a night like tonight they'd be hungover and groggy, especially if we struck while they slept. They did not expect anyone to try and stop them, confident that they had managed to snatch everyone who would come looking, that no one even knew they existed, let alone what they were up to.

But I knew. Sara knew. And we would bring all the fires of Salerah to this cursed place and cleanse it of their evil.

SARA

Orn had wanted me to sleep, but even with wards in place there wasn't any way I was going to let myself relax until he was safe in my arms. I kept holding my breath to listen better, to pick out the sounds of the night and find any thread that might need pulling. But all was still and calm, the storm finally spent and no great calamity striking to crack through the soft sounds of the night.

Even so, every moment he was gone was torture, my mind conjuring horror after horror, growing more certain with every minute that passed that something had gone wrong, that Orn was in trouble, that he needed me. I was torn between staying at our snug camp in case he *did* return safe and sound, and sneaking out to do some scouting of my own. My instinct was to get close to that encampment so that if he needed me, I was already there.

I'd bitten my lips raw in my agitation, standing and striding to the edge of the skirt of boughs hiding our camp, hand already raised to brush the snow-laden branches aside, only to turn around and return to my rolled-up bedroll to resume my wait.

For all my careful listening, I never detected any sounds to warn me of Orn's return. When he parted the thick branches and ducked inside I squeaked and fell backwards onto the thick bed of dried pine needles. *I suppose that was why he was so confident he'd be able to sneak in and out easily,* I thought as I righted myself. It was criminal, that someone so large would be able to move so godsdamned *quietly.*

"Sweet Delenaa, Orn," I muttered as he helped me up. "You'll have to teach me how to move like that."

He shrugged, his cheeks coloring beyond the blushing from the cold. "It's all the blood song," he told me, taking my hand and pulling me down with him so that I was seated in his lap. "Normally I'm a bumbling fool." He curled himself around me, holding me tight and burying his face in my hair, breathing deep. He was quiet for long moments, and while I enjoyed a good cuddle, this one in particular felt...odd.

I squirmed until my arms were free, covering Orn's big hands with my own. "What happened, honey?"

He made a strange noise, low in his throat and somewhere between a growl and a whine. "Nothing, really. They're careless, barely keeping a watch and too busy getting drunk and celebrating to pay any attention to their surroundings."

Chill acid settled in my stomach. "Could...could you tell what they were celebrating?"

He stiffened, then pulled me in tighter and pressed a kiss to my temple. "I think your people are still alive, and from things I overheard, are unharmed. But..." he sighed. "But tomorrow night they're doing a ritual, and I think that that's when...when it'll be too late."

"Salerah's fires, that soon?"

I felt him nod. "But it *does* seem like it will be done during full night, and that they all sleep during the day. So I can have a nap and sharpen my axe—"

"You're not going in alone," I snapped, trying to twist to glare at him. "This is *my* coven, Orn. It's my fight far more than it is yours. And just because I'm a woman—"

He swore in his mother tongue, swatting at my thigh. "That has nothing to do with it, little witch. If you were a man I'd be just as nervous. It's not your ability that's in question, it's mine." He paused, puling in a shuddering breath. "What if I can't keep you safe? What if I let you down and something happens to your coven, and you hate me forever?" I managed to loosen his grip enough to turn and meet his gaze. "Now that I've found you...I don't know if I'd be able to handle it if I lost you."

His over-protectiveness still chafed, but it was hard to stay mad with a great big orc saying such sweet things and looking like the saddest puppy to ever walk Cillure.

"I understand, honey," I told him softly, cupping his broad face in my hands. "But can you set that aside and let me handle myself?"

He looked ready to argue for a moment, nostrils flaring with an agitated huff of breath, but after a moment he sighed and nodded sadly.

"Aye. But if the worst happens and I have to turn to necromancy you have no one but yourself to blame, little witch."

I laughed, kissing him hard. "Deal."

CHAPTER FIFTEEN

The Wound Is Cleaned

SARA

By dawn I'd been more than ready to put an end to the group who'd stolen my coven. Between what Orn had related to me and what I'd seen of them myself it was obvious they were a blight on this world. Their lair made my skin crawl, something slimy and cold and made of pure dark slithering through the back of my mind every second I spent in the horrid cave they'd made their home. It felt like frostbite, like an infection, and even if I didn't know *exactly* what to do to stop it, I knew that when you had a wound going south, you removed all the rot and scrubbed it clean.

The temple they'd erected in the back of the cavern reeked of copper and sulfur, and I was filled with a sharp kind of gratitude that Orn was with me, a blazing-hot and solid presence as my side.

Well, figuratively speaking. In the literal sense, he was actually ahead of me, his battle axe bared, its razor-sharp edge catching the dim light in silver flashes as he swung it and added arcs of crimson to the metallic glints off of his weapon. He was howling something in his native language, his words loud and clear despite the heavy workout he was giving himself. I smiled, thinking fondly about what a sexy little murder machine my man was.

I lowered my gaze to the compass I'd created outside the cavern's entrance—this one neater and stronger than the hasty one of my escape—following the pine needle as it spun in the herb-infused water to the goal I'd directed it to: my coven. The fact that it was pointing so steadily gave me hope. If they'd all been dead, it would have spun aimlessly. So at least one other person besides me was still alive.

I traveled deeper and deeper into the rank cave, the sound of violence drifting over to me from distant twisting corridors bored into the stone walls. I'd stopped focusing on Orn, and his rampage had moved elsewhere in that time. I entered a particularly large cavern and came across an altar, its energy so foul that I was overwhelmed. I bent in half, barely managing to avoid getting my sick all over myself. Once my stomach was empty I stood back up straight, spitting and wiping at my mouth with a wince. I took a swig of water, swishing it around and then spitting that out, too.

The altar was on the smaller side, shrouded in darkness, but it felt like it pulsed and loomed, pressing beyond the physical bounds of the thing to take up the whole room. Whatever darkness this was an altar to, it was deeply wrong, a level of unnatural I would never have guessed was possible before standing in this room. I noticed that the stone platform it rested on was stained liberally with old bloodstains, the rock so saturated it felt like it should still be weeping crimson. I shuddered, pointedly averting my gaze before I got too good of a look at what the wet-looking lumps scattered in offering were.

The compass needle swayed gently off to my left, to the side of the altar, and I edged closer, searching the rock wall for a door, or a cutout—something that would lead me to where my coven was being held. But it was solid, rough-hewn blankness refusing to give way to answers no matter how closely I looked.

I followed the needle to the exact point it was oriented towards, putting my hand on the stone, and was surprised to find that the seemingly solid wall fizzed under my palm. I grinned.

I set the compass on the ground a little distance away, kneeling and slipping my pack off my back to rifle through it and assemble the reagents I'd need. Herbs and tinctures that opened the eyes (including the invisible third eye), that removed shadows, that illuminated what was dark. I ground everything into a powder with my small mortal and pestle, the sharp astringent scent a welcome reprieve from the other smells assaulting me. I then murmured words of power, the keys that would let the door I'd made work. It was difficult without Lena close by to lend me her strength, but I managed it without too much trouble.

As the last word tore free from my numb lips I took a handful of the powder and blew it out into the air, watching it scatter and trickle over the rock wall. The powder ghosted over the rough stone, sparking and popping along all that it touched. The wall began to look less solid, rock melting away like mist under the sun, revealing a lattice of branches and saplings lashed together into a grid spanning the entirety of the revealed opening. And beyond, barely visible beneath the weak, fitful spitting of a mostly-dead torch, eleven lumps huddled together among the filthy straw and human waste.

My knees went weak, a sob ripping from my tight throat. Every one of the lumps turned up to look at me at the sound, some eyes hollow and dark-ringed, some of the skin waxen and too pale, but all alive.

"Sara?" Mother Tonn croaked, her bottom lip splitting from just that one word; they all looked dehydrated, lips pale and flaking and cracked. Her chin wobbled, precious tears welling in her dark eyes. "Sweet Delenaa, *no*. I'd so hoped they wouldn't get you, too."

I shook my head, blinking away tears and stepping closer to their prison. "I'm not captured, Mother. I'm here to rescue you."

"But how?" a younger blond witch with large doe eyes named Callie asked. "There's so many of them. And they have the aid of their...of that *thing*."

A particularly sharp scream pierced the air, followed by a bellow of rage and a faint wet spatter. My coven all shrank back, huddling even closer together than they'd already been. The Mothers all began murmuring a prayer.

I laughed nervously, fiddling with my coat buttons. "Well, I'm not alone. I...I met someone while I was wandering around looking for help. And...he's *very* helpful." I swallowed, almost tearing a button loose from the intensity of my nerves. I wanted so badly for them to accept Orn. But now that I was staring this moment full in the face, I realized I was also nervous that they wouldn't accept *me*, knowing I was an orc's mate.

Squealing and growling floated down the tunnel towards us and I winced, my coven backing as far away from the bars of their cage as they could, eyes wide and faces somehow going even more pale.

"Sara, child, you must *run*," Mother Frannie hissed. "Whoever your companion was, I think he has not been successful. Please, these people are very dangerous—"

Her voice failed her when a roar shivered the air, followed by pounding footsteps. Some of my coven began weeping, moaning that the worst torture they'd endured was that the horrors wouldn't stop coming.

My face flamed. I knew that roar. I even knew the steps, despite only having him in my life a few days.

Orn slid into the cavern, eyes blazing and both sweat and blood spattered over his olive green skin. Somehow he'd lost his shirt, and the tight braid I'd woven his long black locks into was coming loose, wisps of hair flying wild around his head and sticking to his damp skin. He was terrifying, but he was also beautiful, and I was in awe.

With a flick of his wrist a hatchet went flying through the air, striking the hideous altar with a grinding sound and a squeal that was suspiciously organic. Something cracked, and then the altar was on fire. Purple flames licked over the surface, consuming everything, despite much of it being inflammable, until it was a pile of bitter-smelling ash on the floor.

Before I could address that, or any of my other concerns, Orn was on me, hoisting me into the air by my waist and pressing his body against mine. He claimed my slack mouth in a hard, desperate kiss, and I couldn't help but lean into it, relishing the sensory contrast of soft, sweet lips and hard tusks. A large hand gently fisted my curls at the nape of my neck, and despite myself I moaned, legs wrapping tight around his hips.

One of the Mothers cleared her throat, and I gently pushed Orn away from me and eased myself down to the floor. Orn looked furious, his wild eyes darting to the frightened coven as he growled deep in his chest. It was such a low sound I felt it more than heard it.

Smoothing my clothes and hair back into place, I swept a hand over Orn's terrifying form and attempted a smile. "Everyone, this is the companion I mentioned." I grabbed his arm and held it, heart in my throat. "His name is Orn, and he's really very sweet, I promise!"

No one in the cage looked like they believed me. I stifled a sigh and let Orn go. "So it went well?" I asked him, digging around in my pack for more reagents. "What happened to your shirt?"

He snorted. "It couldn't keep up. Weakness must be left behind, when the blood song calls." He lifted his huge battle axe, twirling it like it weighed nothing. "The cult is no more. I will do a final sweep while you finish up here, but I can only hear us, now, in these caves." He flashed me a feral grin. "The scent of wrong already fades."

I paused, smiling up at him as I pulled my basic lockpicking spell out from what I'd brought. "Thanks for taking care of that, honey," I said, realizing too late my mistake.

Orn loosed another growl, this one louder, and scooped me

up into a bridal carry faster than my eye could track. I squeaked, clinging to his neck by instinct. He kissed me again, hard, then began to kiss and nibble my jaw, my neck, hitting all the spots that lit me up and turned me on as if he could somehow see them. Maybe he could—this blood song thing was wild stuff.

"Orn!" I gasped, grabbing his head and doing my best to hold him still. "Focus, big guy."

"I *am* focusing, sweetness," he smirked, easily overpowering me and resuming his searing kisses. I scoffed, trying again to restore order.

"I'll never call you 'honey' ever again if you don't put me down this *instant*, Orn!"

That finally got to him. He stopped his ministrations and set me down, pouting and looking like a mistreated puppy. I swatted at his arm, refusing to fall for it. "Behave yourself or I'm sending you outside, mister. Am I clear?"

"Aye, dove," he grumbled. After a moment he seemed to collect himself a bit and hefted his axe onto one shoulder, the thick muscle bulging with the effort in a way that was distinctly delicious. "Shall I free your folk, then?"

"You can't!" Mother Tonn shouted, shuffling just a little closer and pointing at the bars of their cell. "They're spelled. Touching them stills the heart and sends the soul to their foul god." I shivered, backing away from the innocent-looking lattice. *I guess that means my lockpicking spell is useless,* I thought. I had to spread the thick paste over the lock in order for it to work.

Orn considered the bars, his free hand stroking over his chin and rasping the stubble there. "How far to one side can you manage to get without touching the bars?" he asked them.

"I'm...not sure..." Mother Tonn said slowly. "But we can try and see?"

Orn nodded. Once everyone was packed tightly on the right side of the cell he examined the empty space critically, his dark eyes darting between the empty side and the full side. He grabbed my arm and guided us both back a few steps. "Cover your faces," he told my coven. They did, too weak and curious to protest. And then he was moving, swinging his huge axe in an arc and sending it flying at the bars in front of the empty section of cell. Witches squealed and gasped, huddling still closer, but his aim was true.

The bars were no match for that axe, no matter how strong their curse was. Wood splintered and flew through the air, following the path of the axe and littering the dirty floor. A high-pitched ringing filled the room, and then more of the evil presence filling the cavern ebbed away, the space immediately brighter and more open. Orn retrieved the hatchet he'd used to destroy the altar earlier and used it to widen the hole he'd made. Then he strode in and hefted his axe back up onto his shoulder. He nodded at the wide eyes and slack faces turned up at him. "Ladies," he said, tilting his head in a respectful nod.

"I like him," Brekka declared, and at my best friend's words the tension broke, everyone laughing, some until they were crying and having trouble breathing.

Orn stood close behind me, his arms wrapping around me and holding me tight to his feverishly hot body. My coven slowly trickled out of their cell, joining us in the main cavern chamber. In the improved lighting of the main cavern I was horrified at the state of them; the dimness of the cage had hidden much of their condition, it turned out. I pulled away from Orn and jumped into action, ripping into my pack and pulling out the food and water we'd packed and handing it around to my fellow witches.

I tended to the wounded while the others ate, my heart breaking at what they must have been through for the last few days to be left in this condition. I felt so guilty, knowing I'd been cozy and safe and getting the best sex of my life while awful things were happening to the eleven women who'd become my family in so many ways.

Once everyone had been seen to, Mother Tonn came over and sat beside me. She'd always been most like a mother to me. Her pale hand clasped mine, stilling my nervous fingers, which had been mindlessly picking at a loose thread on my sleeve. "You'll unravel the whole seam at this rate, my dear heart," she said softly, her cool fingers closing tighter over my hand, pouring soothing into me.

"You needn't feel guilty, Sara."

My throat spasmed, tears rushing to my eyes. As if he could smell them, Orn's head snapped up from being bent over his weapons, which he'd been cleaning and sharpening. I gave him a weak smile, nodding at Mother Tonn with my chin. His eyes narrowed, but he stayed where he was. It may have been my imagination, but it seemed like the whet stone was rasping against steel louder than it had been.

Once I'd gotten my feelings under control, I cleared my throat. "How'd you know?" I croaked. It was useless denying it.

"Brekka let me know. And I daresay I know you well enough to guess, even if she hadn't." She loosed a hacking cough that immediately made me nervous, and I dug around for the medicinal lozenges that I always carried when I foraged. Mother Tonn took it gratefully. "Like I said, you have nothing to feel guilty about. You did what you had to to get us help, and knowing you, that young man had to hold you back bodily to stop you from striking out on your own in that blizzard."

I grinned sheepishly. She wasn't too far off from the truth. "Well, I still—I wasted *some* time." *With Orn,* I almost said, but the words wouldn't come, because they were a lie. I never would have been able to free my coven without him, but beyond that...Well, he felt too important to *me,* to my life, to call even our most gratuitous sex a waste.

Mother Tonn smiled knowingly, squeezing my hand before releasing it and resting them delicately in her lap. "I must admit, the orc mate *did* surprise me," she said softly.

My head whipped around to stare at her full in the face. But there wasn't any of the judgment I'd been worried about reflected in her pale blue eyes. She grinned at me, winking saucily. "Fear not, dear one. No one will begrudge you the mate bond. And *especially* not when we have him to thank for our freedom and our lives. This coven owes that man a debt, and the least we can do to repay it is to accept you both with open arms."

"Good," Orn growled, flopping down on my other side and scooping me up to sit in the cradle of his crossed legs. "Because I have been mightily concerned with how I'd honor my word to Sara to help protect you all if you wound up hurting her."

I expected Mother Tonn to be offended, but she just chuckled, shaking her snowy head. "Goodness, you Orcish folk are so *serious* about your mates." She reached over and patted his knee. "You've nothing to fear from us...Orn, was it?"

My fierce mate nodded, idly combing through my hair with his clawed fingers, carefully picking the knots that had wound themselves into my hair loose. I sagged back against him, the weight of my dread lifting all at once and leaving me feeling light as air, and a little dizzy.

Mother Frannie and Kelli soon joined us, then Brekka, then Litha, until the entire coven was gathered around us, asking Orn and I questions—about how we'd met, how we'd come to realize we were mates, about Gehyta. But there was only so much they could avoid the most important questions.

"So how bad is the hamlet?" Litha asked, dread creeping into her soft voice. "We were already caged and hooded by the time we heard—we heard crashes. And smelled smoke."

"There's not much left," I said, meeting each devastated pair of eyes in turn. "I'm so sorry. But by the time I returned from foraging—"

No one's eyes were dry, and some of the younger witchlings began to sob in earnest, but the Mothers managed to keep enough composure to try and get the group calm. "It's alright, witchlings," Mother Frannie soothed, patting shoulders and backs as much as her two arthritic hands could manage. "We've met hardship before, and we'll do it again, aye?"

Orn leaned closer to me, his warm breath tickling my ear. "Would it cause offense if I asked them to stay with us at my cabin?" he murmured.

I stiffened, his question hitting me like a bolt of lightning. "What do you mean?" I asked, wanting to be certain I'd heard him right.

I felt him shrug. "Well, there's not much space right now, but the cabin itself should be able to fit them all, or at least the ones in worse shape." He kissed just under my ear, his lips feather-light on my sensitive skin. "But there's also the barn, and Gehyta only needs a wee bit of it. I'd have to insulate it a bit more, in case there's another storm before spring comes—"

"What about you?"

"I'll be wherever you are, sweetness," he said, kissing me again. "Even if you decide to bunk in the outhouse—"

I swatted his arm. "You don't even *have* an outhouse, you mad thing!"

"Hypothetically, then. I'd lie down in the muck and then you could lie on top of me. Keep you out of the filth and I get to rest using your gorgeous body instead of a blanket. Actually, now that I think about it…"

"I am *not* sleeping in a latrine, Orn!" I hissed. Then I cleared my throat, looking up at my ragged little coven. "We've got a plan!" I told them.

Once I had their full attention I explained what Orn and I had just discussed, and to my relief most every thin, dirty face turned toward us looked pleased and hopeful.

It was decided—we'd rescue what we could from the rubble, rest, and then move along to our new lodgings. And once spring came to the mountains, we would rebuild.

CHAPTER SIXTEEN

Epilogue

ORN

Three Years Later

"Oy, move your great green arse!"

I rolled my eyes, hefting my hay bale higher so that I could let Brekka pass behind me with her pail of fresh milk. "Will you never show me any kindness?" I teased.

She snorted. "Maybe if you and your mate weren't so godsdamned *loud* all night long, I'd be in a better mood."

I laughed. "Alright, fair. And sorry, Brekka. We don't *mean* to do it—"

"But you're too busy trying to see who can fuck whose brains out fastest, I know. Like I said, I can *hear* it."

"Hopefully not too much longer," I added, my face hot with the embarrassment of being caught. But unable to stop my chest from puffing out with pride. I *was* very good at making my mate scream with pleasure, after all. And what was more of a boast than that? "Our cabin's nearly done, now."

If I wouldn't have made sure the rest of the coven was taken care of first, we wouldn't have had to torture them for so long with our...nocturnal athletics. But I'd insisted, and Sara—ever the kind and generous soul—hadn't fought me on it. So ours was the last to be finished in the hamlet that had sprung up around my once-lonely cabin.

I adjusted my grip on the bale of hay I carried and coughed nervously. "It's not...it's not *really* a problem, is it?"

Brekka laughed, but not unkindly. "No, you great big dear. Truth is, more often than not I can barely hear you over the sound of my lady-love wailing away..." Her gaze went soft and sweet. "Salerah's fires, I hope she gets over that cold soon."

I chuckled, returning her affectionate goodbye, then continued on to the expanded barn. I dropped the bale just inside the doors, then went back out and over to the pen, where Gehyta was doing her best to keep the goats, Ruff and Tumble, from picking on our sweet dairy cow, Maisy. At the sight of me at the fence my dear aerlanis bleated, her short tail waggling sweetly, and left the goats to their mischief to greet me.

"Hello, my little queen," I murmured, rubbing her velvet-soft nose and scratching through the silky locks of her long neck. "Are you having trouble with your subjects, again?"

She huffed, butting my chest gently, and I chuckled, scratching behind her ears to try and ease her stress. The goats kept her *mighty* busy.

While I was scratching Gehyta's ears, the long locks on her back stirred, something moving quickly beneath them, and soon Lena had was on top of my aerlanis' head, gently nosing at my hand for her own scratches. I laughed, obliging the little snake, her tiny black eyes closing and her delicate forked tongue tasting the air and my skin. "How do you manage to hold onto Gehyta without any limbs, little one?" I mused.

"She says she is very strong, and that is how. Naturally," a sweet voice said behind me, my heart soaring in my chest at the sound.

I spun to behold my beautiful mate and daughter, my smile becoming beaming. "My loves!" I called, leaving the animals to their games and meeting the two people who held my heart and soul in their small hands.

They both returned my smile, Aora's revealing the wide gap in the front where her baby teeth had fallen out recently. *"Pacha!"* she said — "father" in her mother tongue, she'd told me, bringing me to tears. Her large brown eyes gleamed in the bright light, the blue of the sky reflected in the gleam of her deep brown skin. She came from a remote people on the southern shore of Cillure, far beyond where I'd ever been. Mother Tonn had been gone for months fetching her, but as soon as she'd caught sight of the neglected child, she'd known the long journey was more than worth it.

She had been retrieving a part of our large, messy family, after all.

"Pacha, guess what!"

I lifted Aora into the air and perched her on my hip. She was growing quite tall, but was still thin from her years of malnourishment, and hardly weighed a thing. "What is it, my girl?"

"Morra says she's going to set it up for me to find my familiar, and soon!" she crowed, her little legs kicking me in her excitement. *"I'm so excited!"*

I laughed, tucking a loose tendril of her kinky-curly hair behind her ear. We'd have to redo the twisted knots that covered her scalp soon, I noted. "Do you have any idea yet of what it will be?"

Sara shook her head, one hand plucking a dried blade of grass from our daughter's long dress while the other snaked behind me and grabbed my ass. I managed to avoid jolting, our years of doing exactly this having trained it out of me, but I could not stop the heat that bloomed all over my face. "We don't go into our vision ceremony for our familiar with any hopes or expectations. Isn't that right, lovey?"

Aora nodded, beaming at Sara. "Exactly, *morra!"* She turned to me, rolling her large eyes. "Obviously, *pacha."*

I laughed, hugging her close. "Of course. Forgive this old man his forgetfulness—"

Sara swatted my arm with a snort. "'Old man.' As if you are ancient instead of barely into your thirties."

"Have you heard my knees in the mornings, lately? Sounds like ice cracking during the spring thaw—"

"Sorry to interrupt, my dears," a soft voice interjected from behind Sara, and we both startled at the sudden appearance of Mother Tonn. Being a witch rather than a mage, she wasn't *supposed* to be able to teleport…but in the three years I'd known her, I'd come to wonder. "But we have a visitor. He insists on seeing Orn. He says he knows him…from the Fenns."

My stomach dropped, ice slushing through my veins. "The…the Fenns?" I repeated, dazed. Aora squirmed, tugging at my hand.

"*Pacha*, you're squeezing too tight!"

I loosened my grip at once, pressing a kiss to her forehead in apology. "I'm sorry, little love." I turned to Sara. "Can you take her? In case it's…" Trouble? Bad news? I had no way of knowing, but I knew that whatever would have brought an Orcish man to find me from all the way in the Fenns wouldn't be good.

"I can, but I'm still coming with," my mate answered, taking our daughter.

"Obviously," Aora added, grinning at her joke.

My instinct was to deny them, to send them far away fast as I could, but I knew all that would come of that would be a heated lecture and an arm sore from all the slaps I'd get for my "hyper-masculine posturing". But in truth, I was relieved that they would be by my side. In this, and in all things.

I steeled myself, taking a deep breath, and followed Mother Tonn to the rough gate we'd erected soon after our return from the cult. At first, all I could make out through the slats was a large figure cloaked in faded gray homespun. But as I neared the figure turned, revealing a face that stopped me in my tracks.

"Lyrosh?..." I breathed, Sara's hand on my back barely registering.

"Orn," my eldest brother returned with a curt nod. "You seem to have made out quite well in the north," he added, throwing me a knowing look and nodding his clean-shaven head at a clump of witches huddled together by the nearest cottage.

"They're not my harem," I growled catching his meaning and settling into a fighting stance subconsciously. "They are my *family*. Sisters and mothers. Only one is my mate, and I will not have you insult her by insinuating something so—"

"Alright, no need to get so testy," Lyrosh interrupted, holding up his palms in supplication. "Now that you say it, you do have a look about you I've seen on other mated orcs. Something...settled. Content."

If Lyrosh and myself had been different men, I would have said that in that moment there was something jealous and wistful in my brother's expression. But there was no way that strong, brave Lyrosh would be jealous of me. It had always been that he was my family's greatest pride, and I their greatest disappointment.

He seemed to shake himself mentally, then drew himself up straighter, his shoulders back and his bold chin high. "I would ask that I join you, Orn."

I blinked, shocked. As if sensing my discomfort, Sara came in closer, leaning her soft warmth into my body, reminding me she was there, and that she could be my strength, if I needed it. Lyrosh tracked her movements, and this time it was clearer— Lyrosh *was* envious of me, and it had something to do with Sara. Was he jealous of my having a mate? *Odd beyond measure*, I thought.

Aloud, I said, "I must ask, brother: what is it that brings you here? And why would you wish to join me here in my exile?"

Lyrosh's posture wilted by the smallest measure, and if I didn't know him so well I would have missed it. "I had a vision.

Several months ago, but it has haunted me ever since. It was so tame, so domestic, but you were there, and with you was a warm golden...presence. It called to me, but I did not see who it may be."

My brow furrowed. "A vision?"

Lyrosh nodded, rolling his eyes, just as dark as my own, but with a hard sharpness to them, like an obsidian blade. "I have never put stock in such silly things as dreams, but something about this one would not be ignored. And when I told our parents of it several weeks ago, they said that I should seek you out and track this presence as best I can. That something cast in sacred gold is always important in a vision."

A pang of longing shot through me at the mention of my parents, and Sara pressed in still closer. I put an arm around her, drawing from her silent support, and took a breath to calm my racing heart. "And you have come here because I was in this vision? Are you not banished now because of your association with me?"

Lyrosh rolled his eyes again. "You were not banished in shame, Orn. You *left*. Of your own volition. *You* called it banishment, but you were always the only one."

I snorted, my arm tightening around my mate and child ever so slightly. "Perhaps, but not a soul fought me, or tried to change my mind. I have never been a true orc, not there, and so the only course was banishment, was it not?"

Lyrosh waved a hand through the air, as if to dispel my words. "I don't wish to re-hash this right now, brother. Will you have me or not?"

"I don't know, I hedged. "I will have to consult the others, take it to a vote, perhaps—"

"Of course, we'd *love* to have you!" Sara interjected, shooting me a look that told me not to object. My protest died on my lips. "You are family, are you not? And so long as you follow our few rules, you are welcome to stay as long as you might need." A sharp pinch to the soft flesh of my inner arm made me jump, but

I nodded along reluctantly.

"Yes, I suppose you can stay, then," I grumbled, feeling a little stung at my mate taking control of the situation away from me like that. But when I looked down at her face, already turned up to me, I could not help but soften. She guided me a little ways away, and leaned in close.

"I'm sorry, honey," she said softly, "I know it was your situation to handle, but it felt...necessary. To let him in. And I know how hard things having to do with your family are for you. Does it bother you a lot, that he's here now?"

I was still a little annoyed, but I considered her words. She was no great prophetess, but she had a knack for feeling out where a stone was meant to lie. And aside from my pride, was there truly a reason to keep Lyrosh away from my home? I sighed, feeling my proverbial hackles lower. "I suppose not," I grumbled, stroking her soft cheek with one finger to soften my words. "But I must warn you that things between me and other orcs are...difficult. So this—well, it might prove disruptive to our peace here."

She nodded, grabbing my hand to nuzzle her face into my palm. When she met my gaze, the saucy look in her eyes had me forgetting all about Orcish hierarchy and customs and familial bonds. "He can try to disrupt the peace," she said softly, her voice both lilting and full of dark promise. "But he'd never manage it. Not with an entire coven at your disposal."

Aora, who had been quiet and doing her best to follow our conversation, nodded and giggled. "No one's more stronger than *morra, pacha*. We'll protect you."

My throat tightened with emotion, the protective flame mirrored in my family's eyes bathing me in a holy kind of warmth. I pulled them to me roughly, holding them tightly in an embrace I poured all my love and thanks into.

"You're right, my starlight," I said to Aora, kissing her cheek. "Lyrosh doesn't stand a chance against you." I kissed my mate next, drinking her in like a parched man drinks down fresh, cool water. She hummed softly, returning my kiss with as much passion as I gave, and my heart flew to nest among the heavens. She was right—no one, not even my brother, would be able to harm this.

I broke the kiss but stayed close, one hand cupping the back of her head. "I love you, Sara. Until the stars fade from the sky."

She kissed me again, Aora making a sound of disgust from her perch on Sara's hip. "And I love you, Orn. *So* much."

And my heart was full.

This note is best read picturing me sweaty and struggling to catch my breath while various things explode and/or catch fire around me

Hey. Hi.

So, let's get into it: parenthood hit me (and my husband) like a freight train; we adore our strange little human, but his care (especially in the early days when he had some digestive issues and shitty doctors) wound up being **a lot** more involved and spoon-intensive. Even the old pros were intimidated by just how much Goblincito needed, and we wound up going through a couple of pediatricians to get him the care he needed and on the mend. I also had a lot of issues postpartum with my hormones, PPD+PPA, as well as raging ADHD symptoms that took MONTHS to sort out. The Hot Mess Express stops for no one, not even my newborn spawn.

And then I rushed getting this out, and it blew up in my face.

It's no one's fault but my own that I did what I did, and I own that. I tried to juggle parenting, being a good partner, an edit for a client, preparing for my first IRL convention (Book Harvest 2025) and getting the last 20% of this novella done all at once, and as a result most of those things were done below my standards, if not outright poorly.

Probably what damned me the most with OatRG is that I skipped my paper edit—where I print out the manuscript and correct it with pen on paper— and forgot (yes, I truly forgot this) that I have a wonderful sensitivity reader and an ARC team who could have helped me out. And I am never, ever, never ever, ever never doing that ever again! The paper edit is a part of my self-editing process for a reason, and that reason is that when it comes to editing my own work, it's the only way I can force my brain to see certain kinds of mistakes. But I thought I'd combed through OatRG enough to get it print-ready without needing the paper edit.

BIG. NO.

So if you saw the original manuscript, I am sorry that I put my name on that and put it out there expecting people to spend their valuable time and money on it. Not only were there far more typos than I would have guessed pre- paper edit, there were also moments of insensitivity in regards to Sara's skintone description in one passage and how I presented orcs. I knew better on both counts, but because I was rushing, I didn't realize that what I had put to page was *so far* from what I had intended that it was, in fact, problematic. But now I *have* edited it properly, taken my time with it, and—most importantly —I got it to my amazing sensitivity reader. I cannot thank you enough, Desi'ree! <3

Since disappointing people is one of my biggest triggers, you can rest easy knowing that I will chew my own arm off before I let myself get this careless again! And for what it's worth, I am *truly* sorry, and have done what I can to make it right. But as always, I value feedback and would be open to hearing any suggestions you might have for ways I can do better (beyond what I've already done). I'm getting an anonymous feedback form set up on my website, but as always my email and DMs are open!

In case you're wondering, I HAVE added the story-within-the-story about the orc pirate captain Garesh and his bratty lady-love to my WIP pile, but that heap is up to the ceiling now and it'll probably be a bit before I can get to it. I haven't decided whether or not there will be a sequel to OatRG, but you likely figured out already that if there is, it'll be with Orn's brother, Lyrosh.

So beyond that, what's next for 'ole Mirandy Sapphs? Well, there's some emotional stuff happening with me that makes it hard to say for certain, but I do have a rough plan for it if I can get my head in a better space.

As of writing this I'm getting back into working on the sequel to *A Light in the Dark* that I've been promising and wrasslin' with for basically three years. I've shied away from it, outlined it to hell and back, and just couldn't figure out anything that felt right, but at this point it's more upsetting to ignore it than it is to look at it and work at it. Yay?

Then I'd like to dive back into *Shameless*, which is the second Drakari book and features Fenris and Ravost (and is thus MM). I had written around 70k words while I was pregnant, but shortly before delivering Goblincito I realized that it was all wrong and a terrible direction for them, so I have to do a loooot of re-writing.

Ready Or Not, the second Interstellar Attraction book (*Hope Like Hell* being 1.5), is also in the works, as I've had a breakthrough regarding both Uraka and Djelani as characters, and what their dynamic is going to look like.

I also have some collaborative things on the horizon: a novella set in a fantasy universe shared with other authors, *Moose Knuckle Boxing* with Carlotta Hughes, and probably a whole bunch of other stuff I'll remember at exactly the point that it's too late to add it here.

As always, if you have questions, concerns, or just want to say hi, slide on into my email, Instagram, or TikTok!

Stinky goblin smooches!
Miranda Sapphire, December 2025

A Pronunciation Guide On How I Say These Things, But As Always Feel Free To Pronounce Things However You Want, Because This Is All Made Up And Meant To Be Fun

Orn (ORN)
   Sara (pronounced like Sarah)
   Lena (LAY-nuh)
   Gehyta (GAY-tuh)
   Mother Tonn (MUH-thurr TUHN)
   Mother Frannie (MUH-thurr FRAN-nee)
   Brekka (BREHK-uh)
   Litha (LITH-uh)
   Aggie (AGG-ee)
   Lyrosh (leer-OHSH)
   Aora (OR-uh)

Thrul'hein (THREWL-hine)
   Kellaides (kell-AY-dees)

setha (SETH-uh)

The Cillurean Religion (the Old Gods)

The core of the old religion centers on Yun'Shaddeh, the great scale, keeper of the balance. All things in the world exist in balance with all other things, and when there is inequality they will always attempt rorto: *a return to this sacred balance. Entropy and chaos exist with this balance; they are not its antagonist.*

The Deities:

- Delenaa (del-LAY-nah)(Feminine): Lady of the dawn, goddess of light, spring, beginnings, births.
- Frichta (FRICK-tah)(Neutral Gender): Liege of the dusk, ruler of night, endings, journeys, and autumn.
- Salerah (sahl-AIR-uh)(Neutral Gender): Keeper of the sun, bringer of summer. Deity of fire, harvest, purification.
- Vitrin (VITT-rin)(Masculine): Keeper of the moon, bringer of winter. God of snow and ice, of dreams and death.

In recent years, a monotheistic religion has begun taking hold in some parts of Cillure. This religion is much stricter in its beliefs and means of worship, and has led quickly to abuse and corruption. Its emphasis on the power of men and the importance of legacy is widely-regarded as its greatest misstep.

The Unmaker worshipped by the cult which steals Sara's coven worships an eldritch-styled mythic being. It is not a true god, but promises power and protection to those who discover it and pray to it.

However, it has no interest in coming through on its promises. It is a devourer of worlds, and to bring it to Cillure's plane would have been the death of everything. So good on ya, Orn!